GW01044180

Currently residing in East Herts, Iain Allsopp was born in Scotland and has previously lived in New Zealand and Australia. Happily married and proud father of two daughters and two grandchildren. This is his first novel.

To the Special Ones – you know who you are.

Brat 24.X.2023

Lawrence

Hugely appreciated that you took the time
to have what for me will be one of the most
memorable lunches of my life.

Very best regards

L. U.

Iain Allsopp

RIPPLESWADE HALL

Or a study on madness

AUSTIN MACAULEY PUBLISHERS™

LONDON · CAMBRIDGE · NEW YORK · SHARJAH

Copyright © Iain Allsopp 2022

The right of Iain Allsopp to be identified as author of this work has been asserted by the author in accordance with section 77 and 78 of the Copyright, Designs and Patents Act 1988.

All rights reserved. No part of this publication may be reproduced, stored in a retrieval system, or transmitted in any form or by any means, electronic, mechanical, photocopying, recording, or otherwise, without the prior permission of the publishers.

Any person who commits any unauthorised act in relation to this publication may be liable to criminal prosecution and civil claims for damages.

This is a work of fiction. Names, characters, businesses, places, events, locales, and incidents are either the products of the author's imagination or used in a fictitious manner. Any resemblance to actual persons, living or dead, or actual events is purely coincidental.

A CIP catalogue record for this title is available from the British Library.

ISBN 9781528987271 (Paperback)
ISBN 9781528987288 (ePub e-book)

www.austinmacauley.com

First Published 2022
Austin Macauley Publishers Ltd®
1 Canada Square
Canary Wharf
London
E14 5AA

Lyrics credit from the song titled "Feelings 4 u" written , performed and produced by Low Deep T for cut&play music, UK.

IN THE ROYAL COURTS OF JUSTICE   PFW-97310 – 42974
QUEEN'S BENCH DIVISION

(1) NATALIE REBECCA FIONA TRELEWYN-DIGBY   The Claimant

-    and –

(2) BARRINGTON OLIVIER WHIBLEY   The Defendant

First Witness Statement of Barrington Olivier Whibley

I, Barrington Olivier Whibley of Willow Cottage, Norton Farm Road, Favering Creechurch, Dorset DT34 3LU will make oath and say as follows:

1. I make this statement in response to legal proceedings that have been issued against me by Natalie Trelewyn-Digby ("NTD").

2. I am a qualified electrical engineer and am a fellow of the Royal Academy of Engineering. My first degree was in civil engineering at Aberyswith University, where I graduated with an upper second in 1967.

3. In view of the nature of some of the allegations that have been made against me I have set out below in some detail how I became an expert in the forensic analysis of fire claims. After graduating I worked at KMT Limited, a long-established engineering practice in the West Country. I worked at that firm from the autumn of 1967 to 1992, just under 25 years. At the beginning of my career I worked as a junior engineer, but after three years I was made an associate and ten years later I became a senior associate, which was the position I held until my departure.

4. From 1975 to 1984 my clients required more and more forensic work from me and I began my practice in fire investigations. This came about primarily as a result of one of our major clients buying up a regional fish and chip shop chain late in 1974. Over the following six years there were nine significant fires in those shops

all related to either alleged defective fryers or ducting. This is a specialised field and as there was no relevant expertise in the West Country at that time.

5.   From early 1985 until 1992 I was head of a separate unit from the main practice, which became known as Forensic Investigations. For most of this time there were three of us; myself, Bill Nially and Teresa Hart, effectively our PA/secretary. The work had steadily grown from the mid-1970s and we had successfully gotten onto the expert panels of various insurance companies, including some Lloyd's syndicates.

6.   The work essentially involved making site visits either during or immediately after significant fires, ranging from small businesses, warehouses to private residences. Our clients were the insurers of the premises that had suffered damage. We covered the whole of the South-West region and it was common for us to be out of the office for three to four days of the week.

7.   Fires leave many clues as to their origin and nature and the sooner you can inspect the site the better. The main issue for forensic examination is that the fire brigade's priority is to put the fire out and then ask questions.

8.   As a result of our success Bill and I were approached in 1992 to join a new company called Dunling & Co. KMT Limited had become less interested in supporting and pursuing the forensic work our team was undertaking and it was therefore agreed that Forensic Investigations would move to Dunling.

9.   We took all of our ongoing work with us and I understand KMT did well out of the deal. With the more positive backing we received at Dunling, Bill and I were able to expand and grow our business and by the time I left Dunling, to become an independent consultant, we had a team of seven. The areas of expertise had also widened so we

took on all property damage work including water damage, subsidence and theft.

10. The reason for becoming a consultant was that I had become disenchanted with all of the administrative and management responsibilities of being the senior member of the team. The clucking puppets that characterise so much of British middle management were a bore. On joining Dunling both Bill and I were made up as partners. With increasing pressure on billing targets, business plans and strategy initiatives I found very little time was being spent doing what I really enjoyed, forensic analysis. Instead of being out on the road three to four days a week I was in the office. In September 1992 it was therefore agreed with the Dunling partners that I would be retained as a consultant – effectively withdrawing from all of the management responsibilities. I was to be paid on an hourly rate for forensic investigation work undertaken on Dunling's behalf.

11. The fire, which is the incident at the heart of the legal proceedings that have been issued against me personally, was a matter referred to me directly approximately six months after I had been working as a consultant. The instructions were sent by Jed Parker, the Claims Manager at Gluckman Insurance Company Limited, someone I had worked with for many years. The reason why I can recall these particular instructions so clearly is that Jed had contacted me directly and this had caused issues as to whether I was being instructed in my independent capacity or whether the instructions were intended to be via Dunling. It took a number of phone calls to establish and agree that these instructions were not for Dunling's account and these instructions were sent to me in my personal capacity as an independent forensic expert. Hence the reason, I assume, that Dunling was not named in these proceedings.

12. Indeed, I can clearly recall receipt of these particular instructions. As I mentioned above, Jed Parker has known me for over 20 years and it was his personal style to first of all telephone to discuss any

new matter he was forwarding. Claims people do things in different ways. Some simply write to you, some email but Jed always called first. The reason I recall this was that it was difficult to say much during this initial call without having seen the papers. The insurance policy and declaration would normally be provided with the initial instructions. Shown to me now and marked "**BOW 1**" is a copy of that original letter of instruction on the fire at Rippleswade Hall.

13.   The other reason I can recall these instructions coming in is that the fire had occurred nearly seven days earlier and it was unusual not to receive papers on such a potential loss within 24 hours of the incident. There did not appear to be any explanation for the delay. Jed knew that time was of the essence in these types of claim and really critical evidence can be lost or destroyed very quickly.

14.   What makes the delay even more peculiar was that this had been one of the key issues with the Cap'n Cod Fish Bar fire in 1984, one of the first large instructions I had received from Jed. That fire had occurred in the early hours of a Sunday morning, discovered at 4:30 a.m. by drunken passers-by. If I can give people one useful tip from all my years of experience in this business it is never live above a chip shop. The owner of the Cap'n Cod Fish Bar in Nether End was a Mr Wistham; a decent, hard-working family man with a wife and two young children. He lived above the shop and his wife and daughter both of whom perished in the fire, and his baby son suffered second degree burns and severe smoke inhalation. What struck me immediately with the Cap'n Cod matter was that there was no smoke alarm in the flat, Mr Wistham had assumed the smoke alarm in the shop would be sufficient. The cold reality was that if the drunken locals had not raised the alarm when they did the whole family would have perished.

15.   It was one of the hardest matters I had to deal with. Understandably, Mr Wistham was in no fit state to speak with me and his brother-in-law had the sense to appoint a loss assessor on his behalf. They do have their uses. The instructions on this matter came in four days

after the fire. It was clear from the preliminary paperwork this was a total write off but the critical thing was to be able to examine the two fryer units and the ducting, or more precisely what was left of them. All sorts of theories were put forward as to the cause of the fire; including one of the fryers being left on accidentally, one of the thermostats on one of the fryers being faulty, residue in the ducting catching fire and a discarded cigarette.

16. From an early stage, soon after I made my first site inspection, and from the statements made by the attending fire officers, it seemed clear that the seat of the fire was either in, or directly above, the fryer closest to the entrance. The fire had gutted the building and there was significant rainfall soon after the fire was put out. Persons unknown had stolen the burnt out fryers and ducting, presumably for scrap metal, which meant that the critical evidence was either missing or water damaged. Had I been called immediately; the site would have been made secure and the evidence would have been collected and put into safe storage.

17. It should have been possible to quickly establish where the fire started, depending on whether it was the fryer or the ducting that had been the cause of the fire – the fire patterns and spread would have been quite different. The ducting fitted to the ceiling would have burnt very differently to a fire staring in the fryer at ground level.

18. Mr Wistham was still very shaken and distressed when I first met him seven days after the fire. He was able to confirm that the particular Saturday in question had followed a normal routine. He had gone down to the shop at approx. 10:30 a.m. and switched on the fryers for opening at 11:30. Trade was normally slow until just after midday. Mr Wistham did very little pre-cooking, almost everything was cooked to order. This made sense and was common practice as it cut down on wastage. Mr Wistham had originally been confused as to whether he had in fact switched on both of the fryers, as Saturday lunchtimes were not usually busy and he would generally have only switched on one fryer, which was the one

furthest from the entrance. He was adamant that he normally only switched on the fryer nearest to the entrance on a Friday and Saturday night. Business was unexceptional that day and he closed at 2:30 p.m. turning off "both the fryers" and leaving the ducting extractor fans on timer to switch off at 3:00 p.m. Mr Wistham had then gone upstairs to have an early tea and a nap before opening again at 5:00 p.m. – he normally stayed open on a Saturday until 11:30 p.m.

19.   Mr Wistham went down to the fry bar at 4:30 p.m. and turned on all three fryers. Interestingly he commented that the fryer on the left-hand side of the range, left if you are standing behind the range looking out towards the customers on the other side, still seemed unusually warm. This of course immediately raised the question of whether the thermostat and on/off switches were working properly. It had been nearly eight months since the last service and the range was nearly six years old. It was newly purchased by Mr Wistham when he opened Cap'n Cod.

20.   The reason why this was important was that the insurers of Mr Wistham paid out just under £250,000 and would be seeking a recovery from whichever party was discovered to be responsible for the fire. In situations such as this there are a number of possible targets including the fry bar manufacturer, the thermostat manufacturer, the ducting manufacturer, the installers and the company paid to service and clean the equipment.

21.   So my task was to make investigations and define, in so far as I was able, what the cause of the fire had been. As mentioned in paragraph 16 (above), in this case parts of the fry bar range and ducting appeared to have been taken, no one knew for sure by whom. The attending fire brigade, without any evidence or witnesses, had referenced the fact that just outside the village a group of travellers had made a semi-permanent camp, since which time there had been a marked increase in petty crime. It struck me as odd that the fire service had stated this to be the case, but the Fire Report, completed

after the fire brigade's attendance at any fire, was for Home Office statistical purposes, not for forensic investigative purposes.

22. I have no particular issue with travellers but there is no doubt in this case that whoever took the fire damaged ducting and parts of the fry bar range had either inadvertently or deliberately taken the critical evidence that was so important to my investigations.

23. My suspicions were mildly aroused when Mr Wistham commented that he guessed that it made it difficult to turn down his insurance claim, if there was no hard evidence of foul play and therefore the insurance company would be looking to pay out and get the matter closed. I was about to say that this may not necessarily be the case but stopped myself. Instead, I said that it may be an important factor in the insurer's declinature if anything untoward were discovered during the detailed process of considering the recovery options. Mr Wistham fidgeted and asked what I meant by that.

24. The key point, which I have somewhat laboured to make, is that the earliest possible involvement of the forensic team at the site is essential. The TV is full of criminal investigation teams at murder scenes and my work is similar, perhaps a little less glamorous.

25. It is with great clarity and detail that I can recall the three visits that I made to Rippleswade Hall:

    (1) on 15 December 2013 when my first visit was foreshortened by the snow storm;
    (2) on 9 April 2014 my second visit when I made a detailed inspection of the fire damage; and
    (3) on 21 June 2014 when I made a personal visit to attend a dinner party.

26. NTD lives at Rippleswade Hall, a mock Tudor/Gothic style manor house, built by her great-great-grandfather John Trelewyn over 120 years ago. Most local people are not even aware of the existence of

the property as it is 1.2 miles down a twisting tree lined private drive off the Chidbury Caundle to Mudford road. The entrance is marked by a stone gateway with iron gates. The driveway is covered in loose white stone, larger than shingle, but similar to look at from a distance. The first quarter mile of the drive twists through a wooded area and then becomes tree lined on both sides until you reach the Hall. At the point where the drive becomes tree lined there are raised banks on either side and the trees had been planted on top of the banks. This had the effect (I assume intended) as though you were driving through a tunnel. My first visit was in December. By the time I left it was dark and there were hundreds of white lights wrapped around the bare trees, which created a magical effect as I drove back to the main road through the sparkling tunnel and snow began to fall for the first time that winter.

27.   From my time on subsidence claims I knew something about trees and these were magnificent Cherry trees and I began to wonder if special soil had been brought in to create the banks onto which they had been planted. It intrigued me, as did many things to do with Rippleswade Hall.

28.   The drive opened out approx. 100 metres from the Hall, so that as you left the tunnel you saw in its panoramic glory for the first time the resplendent Rippleswade Hall. It became quickly apparent that NTD's grandfather had great vision; as the effect of the avenue of Cherry trees would have taken decades to grow up and in spring bloom they created a floor of petals that ran all the way up the drive. One of the measures of how well Rippleswade Hall had been designed was the fact that there had been no major alterations or additions since it was first built. A point that I was later to learn was a source of great pride to the family.

29.   The frontage of the Hall is a mixture of Tudor/Gothic and the three floors seem imposingly tall but yet somehow proportionate. It is an "E" shaped building with three abutting frontages; one on each side

and one in the middle being the main entrance, the two recessed areas having ornate borders.

30. The entrance to the Hall is particularly impressive. There is a large wooden front door made of Yew (unusual I would say) and this opened into a large square hallway with chequered black and white tile flooring. The main staircase, in Oak, began at the far wall of the hall and impressively climbed two sides of the hallway. A Yew door and Oak staircase, I would say that was unique.

31. In the hallway hung a number of very fine oil paintings. Although I could not be sure I would have said they were by William Nicholson, a variation on The Lustre Bowl with Green Peas from 1911 I think. It is an exquisite piece. Opposite that painting, on the adjacent wall, hung what appeared to be an early version of The Viceroy's Orderly. Two exquisite paintings which were of no little historical importance.

32. Perhaps unfortunately, as an adjuster, my immediate thought was whether these paintings were adequately insured. William Nicholson has become a not insignificant figure in modern British art, for some odd reason often overshadowed by his son Ben.

33. There were a number of pieces of furniture in the hallway, specifically two eighteenth century tables. Upon both of which were large glass vases with elaborate flower displays. My initial reaction was that these were silk flowers but upon closer inspection I realised that both vases were full of fresh flowers. They were identical blue and white arrangements in both vases, lilies, thistles, allium, nasturtiums and green foliage. Lilies can have a rather pungent smell as they age but the arrangements had a delicate and sweet smell and you could see that the stamens had been carefully removed.

34. The overall effect of the hallway was one of understated opulence. An apposite way of describing Rippleswade Hall. Every piece seemed proportionate but it did not feel cluttered. I have attended many expensive residences in my time and one thing I do know is

that money does not buy good taste. Indeed, in many cases it is true that wealth is wasted on the rich. So many properties are cluttered and ill thought out; this was definitely not the case with Rippleswade Hall.

35.   Various rooms led off from the main hallway including the large kitchen, dining room, two day rooms and what was called The Stoop; a study, come bar, come billiards room. A rich man's playroom. As NTD explained, nearly ten years ago the kitchen had been gutted and completely refitted. The only other major works that had been done at Rippleswade Hall had been the addition of en suite bathrooms to certain of the bedrooms on the first floor. These were the only works undertaken since the Hall had been first built. I sensed from NDT there was a little regret, as though it had been a great sense of pride to be able to say that nothing had been significantly touched or altered since it had been built.

36.   This new, modern kitchen was beautiful, no doubt about it. With precisely the same care and attention with which the Hall itself had been designed and built. The smallest detail of this kitchen had been thought through. From the French bureau that housed a significant collection of cookery and wine books, to the inlaid display cabinet that housed a collection of espresso cups (at least 40 cups and saucers). The fitted cabinets were in French Oak, with exquisite black with grey speckled marble worktops. All the handles, trimmings were in brushed steel. On one wall there was a recessed fireplace and at the end of the kitchen nearest the entrance a large twelve seater farmhouse table and two trestles. One along each side of the table upon which to sit. It was more striking than any kitchen I had ever seen in *Homes & Gardens*. There was a French door, opposite the fireplace, that led out onto a patio on which there were various clay pots containing numerous large herbs. To the left of the fireplace was a door that led into an old-fashioned north facing pantry, more than a cursory nod to the original design. I was surprised when NTD explained that the kitchen had been true to the

original layout, just modernised. It was easy to imagine the fire alight in winter and the French windows opened wide in summer.

37. On a table next to the French dresser was a TV and next to it a CD/radio with a small orderly stack of CDs. This was the only part of the kitchen that did not quite seem to fit and I think NTD saw my reservation and explained that this room was the hub of the house. So many of the rooms almost completely unused – but here was the heartbeat of the house. I do not recall on which visit that discussion took place.

38. My first visit to Rippleswade Hall plays out like a sepia film, mid-December on a bitterly cold afternoon. It was one of those dark winter's days that never seems to properly light up. As though a dimmer switch has been turned to low for the day. NTD herself had opened the front door and welcomed me with a smile that was neither too forced nor lacking in a little warmth. She was a striking lady and I immediately thought of Audrey Hepburn. It was her simple but elegant style rather than a direct comparison to Ms Hepburn. Her hair was neatly tied back and she had a coral cashmere jumper draped over her shoulders. Her dark complexion was emphasised by her jet black eyes, not brown but black. They were strikingly beautiful and mesmerising. The first thing anyone would mention about NTD, if they were asked to describe her, would be her eyes. I would guess that NTD was in her mid 50's but I am not a good judge of these things — it would not entirely surprise me if NTD was 65 or 43, but on balance I would have said she was in her early to mid fifties.

39. We went straight into the kitchen and I recall pausing very briefly to note a large Christmas tree in the hallway decorated only with small white lights that were slowly going on and off. I can recall no other Christmas decorations either on the tree or anywhere else in the Hall that I saw on that visit.

40.　　NTD beckoned me to sit at the table in the kitchen with a hand movement and she then put on the kettle and took out cups and saucers. She asked if I took milk and sugar. She returned to the table whilst the kettle boiled and her walk reminded me of our aging cat. Almost just a little too slow, but languid and elegant. It were as though she did not expend one bit more energy than she needed to. Whilst she made the coffee I could not help but notice a photograph of her above the fireplace.

41.　　There are many framed photographs in Rippleswade Hall and a reasonable number of them are of NTD. There was no getting away from the fact that she had been a rare beauty. The photo of her to which I refer was a black and white photo, framed in solid silver and sat on the right hand side of the mantel piece above the kitchen fire. I have not seen that photo since my second visit. The mantel piece was quite high, so the picture was only just below head height and in it she stood by herself, with a jumper draped over her shoulders, much as it had been when I first met her. She must have been 18 or 19 in the photo and had a perfect complexion and this was emphasised by the acuity of the picture being in black and white. She was wearing a pearl necklace and matching pearl earrings. She was standing at 45 degrees to the camera and her head was a little bowed and to the side. Her eyes gazed directly into the camera so she looked straight at you – it was a striking photo for a number of reasons. I could not help feeling that even at that age she had already worked out what angles flattered her in photographs. Her eyes had a dreamy, almost sleepy disposition, which gave her a mesmerising quality that only added to her allure. It was as though she had some foreign lineage, but just a little, maybe an Oriental great grandmother. All of these qualities she still had but she was simply older. She had a calmness and confidence that made one just a little envious. It was a striking photograph of an extraordinary young lady but one that hauntingly emphasised the passage of time, as one felt that she could never have looked more beautiful than she did in that photograph. It was from a time long ago, a time that no longer existed except in photos such as this. It was a photograph that made you feel very strongly that you wanted to be able to climb into it. To climb back into that precise moment when NTD was such an exquisitely beautiful young lady. NTD saw that I was looking at the photo but, on this occasion, made no comment.

42. The coffee, unsurprisingly, was some of the best I have ever had. She had made a cafetiere and provided double cream, not milk. A treat that I normally only indulged in occasionally. I commented on how good the coffee was and NTD gave one of her slow knowing smiles. She explained that she had been purchasing the same Colombian coffee beans from the same coffee merchant in Padchester for over 30 years. It was not difficult to see why. She mentioned the coffee merchant and where they were based but the details I could not at the time remember. I also had reason to comment on the black lacquer tray upon which she had carried the coffee. It was more a piece of art than a tray with gold and bronze inlay. Again, she explained that it had been purchased by her grandfather in Saigon and I immediately wondered if that was where her grandfather was from but it did not seem appropriate to ask. I had, after all, made this visit to investigate a fire loss, not to compile her biography or family history.

43. I had certainly spoken to NTD on the telephone on more than one occasion to arrange this visit. She had been pleasant but seemed ever so slightly distracted when we had spoken. Not in a supercilious, disinterested sort of way, just distracted. She was "well to do" is how I think my mother would have phrased it. The reason why I state this here is that approximately 15 minutes after our meeting had started NTD took a telephone call, politely excusing herself saying she was expecting an important call but would only be a few minutes. She had answered the phone in the hallway and I remained in the kitchen but I could easily hear everything she said. NTD has a very clear and resonant voice.

44. It was only later that I considered that the call had been from a relative or close friend of a former member of staff at Rippleswade Hall. When the caller introduced himself to NTD she had responded

by commenting how good it was of them to take the time to call and she had warmly enquired after "dear Dorothy". It was the tone of her voice that I recall; it seemed lowered ever so slightly, and it was warm and sincere. She really did want to know how dear Dorothy was. I do not recall the exact detail nor could I hear the other half of the conversation, but it became apparent there were some sort of financial issues relating to Dorothy. NTD became quite emphatic, they were not to concern themselves with the bills/paperwork/demands – these were to be sent to NTD's accountant and they would be taken care of as "Rippleswade's" mark of thanks and respect for all Dorothy's hard work over the years. Not her, or her family's gratitude, but "Rippleswade's". The caller was told not to worry; everything would be taken care of. When NTD returned into the kitchen she smiled and apologised for the "interlude".

45.   Occasionally, NTD used a word slightly out of context, in an odd or unusual way, which made me think that perhaps a long time ago English had not been her first language. She used the word "interlude" when I think she meant to say "interruption". My fastidiousness on such matters dates back to grammar lessons with Miss Van der Meinnen some 50 years ago. I can still recall quite clearly a number of her lessons and for that reason alone I would suggest she was probably the most influential teacher I had. One particular lesson on the correct and precise use of English remains with me. We were shown a series of pictures and had to describe what was in the picture. I got top marks and Miss Van der Meinnen used my answers as examples of correct answers for the rest of the class. The one picture I can still recall was a cat sitting on a mat. So I wrote: "The cat sat on the mat." However, Celia Brocken had written "A fat black lazy cat wanted to be let in the door." As Miss Van der Meinnen pointed out it was not clear from the black and white picture: (1) what colour the cat was; (2) that there was any door; (3) it was impossible to state the cat was lazy and (4) there was no use of grammar. Whether or not Celia Brocken should have burst into tears is not for now.

46.   I have sat through many hundreds of lessons/lectures/ talks of which I can remember hardly anything at all and yet there are some grammar lessons with Miss Van der Meinnen that I will take with me to my grave. Whilst on detention one Friday afternoon (no games for me that day) and under the supervision of Miss Van der Meinnen she had written on the blackboard "As a seed, am I perhaps also a strawberry?" I think I fell a little more in love with Miss Van der Meinnen that afternoon.

47.   To be fair I suppose we all occasionally use words incorrectly or out of context and it may be that I am being a little harsh on NTD.

48.   As I always did on a first visit with a new client, I went through very carefully the purpose of my visit to Rippleswade Hall, explaining my appointment by her insurers and that my instructions were to make a detailed examination into the cause of the fire, the resulting damage and the operation and response of the insurance policy to this claim. By the questions she asked me it was clear that NTD was an intelligent lady. She made a comment about average. In layman's terms, average is the insurance principle whereby a claim can be reduced if the insured has underinsured their property. A claim will be reduced on a pro rata basis in these circumstances and NTD clearly knew about this. I did think of asking her at the time if there had been some earlier insurance claim at Rippleswade Hall, which was the most obvious explanation for her knowledge on this point, but I did not. Strange, because I normally would have asked.

49.   She explained that with regard to the rooms that had been damaged in the fire, it was terribly difficult to provide any sort of accurate estimates of quantum. There were a number of paintings, pieces of furniture, certain ornaments (including some fine China and silver) that had been in the family for generations and were going to be almost impossible to value. The last detailed valuation and inventory had been undertaken over 40 years ago.

50. One point I do recall is that NTD made no mention whatsoever of her husband, ex-husband, partner, dead husband – not a single word or reference. There were a number of times during that discussion when it would have been appropriate to say something, indeed I made deliberate reference to my wife to see if this elicited a response. As mentioned earlier, there were many framed photographs in various rooms but I cannot recall seeing a photo of NTD with anyone who might have been her husband/partner. On the only other work related visit I recall picking up a photo of NTD with a man about her age and saying something like "Ah your husband?" and as she discretely cleaned the frame of my finger prints and replaced it and she said " No, my cousin," with that beautiful enigmatic smile. The smile said "I know you would like to know a lot more about my personal life, but I am not going to tell you."

51. The preliminary conversation in the kitchen went on much longer than I expected. It is with embarrassment that I must confess that the impending snow-storm that had been forecast to "move slowly westwards" had arrived much sooner than expected. In the dimming light outside looking through the French doors onto the herb garden I became aware that snow was beginning to fall. I commented on this immediately because I knew that I must not delay my departure, and NTD was suitably concerned that she must not detain me. With the fire lit, the kitchen felt warm and inviting like a favourite old pub that you find tucked away in remote villages in the Yorkshire Dales. Not somewhere you particularly wished to hurry away from, certainly not when a snowstorm was approaching.

52. Explaining that I would need to make another visit NTD asked if it would be of any use to quickly review the damaged rooms. Not realising the full size of Rippleswade Hall I agreed, but when it took nearly five minutes to climb to the third floor and to the back of the property I wished I had been honest and said there was no need. Certainly there was a pull both to Rippleswade Hall and to NTD that is not easy to resist and there was the prospect of staying just a little longer with both.

53.   I took two photographs in each of the three rooms and these are shown to me now marked "**BOW 2**". The first two rooms we went into were more badly damaged than I expected; the ceiling in the room in which the fire had started was supported by struts and some temporary patching to make it weatherproof had been carried out on the exterior roof. It struck me then that I must not delay my next visit too long. By the time I had made a quick inspection of the seat of the fire and identifying that the weatherproofing seemed sound, I explained that I needed to leave to try and get home before the snowstorm set it. NTD was understanding and did not seem particularly perturbed that I needed to return.

54.   The third room was clearly one that NTD used, but it was not her bedroom. It was sort of between a study and dressing room I suppose. I did not take measurements but all the rooms were generously proportioned and this room would have been approx. 30 feet square, or thereabouts. NTD referred to the room as we entered as "My retreat" and I think I said something to the effect that I had always had aspirations myself for a study – however this was both more and less than a study. The "Retreat", as I shall refer to it hereafter, was not decorated in keeping with the other two rooms or indeed with Rippleswade Hall generally. To begin with it had a false lower ceiling, which reduced the height of the ceiling by approx. four feet. When I noted this NTD explained that she treasured the lack of head space, she actually felt that she was in a room. It had also been particularly fastidiously decorated with a modern plaster effect on the walls in marbled aubergine, a dark rich burgundy that was dark at floor level but slowly lightened up the wall as it rose so that near to the ceiling the colour was many shades lighter – it had a very purposeful effect. In front of the window was an old oak desk directly over which was a modern glass table on which there was a large laptop and modern lamp. There was a French book cabinet in Walnut, what appeared to be three extracts from the Koran ornately mounted and framed, an Arabic lantern and two small ornate French tables with lamps on them. It appeared to be one of the few rooms in which there were no photographs. The window looked out onto

the back of the Hall but by then it was dark. I could see the snow falling outside so I know the curtains were not drawn.

55.   Perhaps fortunately, this appeared to be the least damaged of the three rooms that formed the subject of the insurance claim. The damage was primarily smoke damage and there was a clear finger mark on the inside of the door where you could see that someone had run their finger along the door to show the layer of smoke residue that had been left. I did warn NTD at the time that smoke damage was often worse than first realised, particularly with regard the three framed items and the French book cabinet all of which would almost certainly need expert cleaning/restoration.

56.   Given that we were in her "Retreat", and this room clearly had a special meaning for her, NTD seemed remarkably sanguine and calm and made only a cursory acknowledgment when I mentioned this. More often than not it is my experience the owner becomes particularly agitated about certain items, sometimes a photograph, sometimes a piece of furniture but usually it was something with significant sentimental value.

57.   We would have spent a total of no more than 10 minutes in the three rooms and my notes were very brief.

58.   It is my normal practice to make a digital recording of the first introductory meeting as this provides an exact record of what is said and I then prepare a written transcript for my records and keep the tape. Rather pedantic, but it has proven useful during my professional career. In my initial wonderment with Rippleswade Hall this had completely passed me by – no recording. I made a mental note that this must be done at the beginning of my next visit. It is primarily to protect myself and is strong evidence of what exactly was, and in some cases was not discussed with the insured.

59.   That first visit was a few weeks before Christmas and the journey home took nearly four hours as the snow set in, causing multiple

delays and difficult driving conditions. But the thing that still sticks in my mind is the drive back down to the road. It was a dark night and the snow, although only just starting, was already earnest. Each of the bare Cherry trees had been wrapped with white Christmas lights and the journey through the "tunnel", if I can call it that, was magical. I did not get out of second gear, I have a four wheel drive, and should have been making time, but it was impossible. I had been tempted to stop the car for a few minutes on the drive and in the "tunnel" but that would have been odd. It was a tunnel of branches, lights, gently falling snow and it was still and tranquil as it so often can be when it snows. One of those serenely magical Christmas moments one experiences only rarely and I knew it at the time and savoured it.

60.   Shown to me now and marked "**BOW 3**" is a letter from me to NTD thanking her for her time and hospitality upon my first visit. On reflection it is most odd and improper that I should sign off that letter "Love Whibley" and I cannot now say or explain why I did that. The letter was written the day after my first visit and I must have been a little stirred still

61.   In the letter I confirmed another appointment would be necessary, as we had discussed. In response NTD telephoned me before Christmas to explain that she was to be away from just after Christmas until early March and that she wished to be present when I attended again. I tried to explain that this would not be necessary and that as long as someone was there who could let me in but I realised this was not going to happen. She said something like "I think it will happen differently". The phraseology was odd but it was clear that I would have to accede to her request so it was agreed that NTD would contact me upon her return to Rippleswade Hall in March and at that time we would set a date. It was immediately after that conversation that it struck me as slightly odd that NTD made no mention whatsoever of to where she was going. Normally you would expect someone to say we are off to Italy or Barbuda or wherever it

is that people go to when they can afford to go away for months. But she said nothing.

62.   **The Second Visit**

63.   The following is a transcript of the conversation that took place between me and NTD on 9 April 2014 in the kitchen of Rippleswade Hall, at the beginning of the second visit and indeed by accident recording almost the whole of that visit.

BOW: This is a recording of a conversation between myself, Barrington Olivier Whibley and Natalie Trelewyn-Digby starting at 09:52 a.m. on Thursday 9 April 2014. This meeting has been arranged both by telephone and by email. The purpose of this visit to Rippleswade Hall is for me, as the appointed agent, adjuster and forensic expert of Gluckman Insurance Company Limited to undertake a site investigation into a fire that occurred on 23 October 2013 and which is now the subject of an insurance claim under the property and contents policy number HNWHC045921-304 taken out by NTD. Now, Mrs Trewelyn-Digby …

NTD: Please call me Natalie.

BOW: Natalie, thank you. You have submitted an insurance claim for the repair, restoration and/or replacement for three rooms and their contents as a result of a fire that occurred on 23 October 2013 on the third floor of the northeast rear wing of Rippleswade Hall.

NTD: That is correct.

BOW: By way of explanation, this is an introduction to the purpose of my visit. I am in the habit of recording this discussion in order that there is a well recorded and documented account of what has been said. Sorry, this all sounds a little formal but we are nearly there.

NTD: Would you like some coffee?

BOW: Yes, thank you; that is most kind.

NTD: Please, you continue and I will make the coffee. (Laughing) For the purposes of the tape Natalie Trelewyn-Digby has left the table and moved over to the far end of the kitchen where she is switching on the kettle and making coffee.

BOW: Yes (chuckles) – very good Mrs Trelewyn-Digby. Yes it does seem a little like a police interrogation, like so many police dramas on TV. Perhaps, if you prefer……. I just need to cover a few more points and then I can switch it off.

NTD: Sorry, I did not mean to be facetious.

BOW: That's quite alright. [in-audible] ….warranted and in order under the circumstances. I have done this for so long that I forget to try and put myself in the position of the insured. It just seems normal to me.

NTD: There we are. Milk, no cream this time I'm afraid, and sugar?

BOW: Milk and one sugar, thank you. There are just a few more introductory points I must cover if I may. As you will be aware from my first letter to you this matter is being investigated under a reservation of rights as the facts are still not well understood, in particular, the cause of the fire. You were informed that you are perfectly entitled to appoint your own representative, either a loss assessor or solicitor if you wished to do so but the costs of such an appointment would not be covered under you policy and would have to be borne by you in any event, whatever the outcome of my investigations. You indicated to me over the telephone, and during my first visit, that you did not intend to appoint anyone but for completeness I am clarifying that your right to do so has been raised and discussed with you. You have understood this point; I am more than happy to…….

NTD: I fully understand.

BOW: Good, well I think that brings me to the end of the formalities and introductory points that I need to cover. May I just say what a beautiful property this is. Truly magnificent.

NTD: You are very kind. As I explained previously it was built by my great-great-grandfather in 1814 and has been the family home ever since. I love this place dearly – thank you.

BOW: I can see how one could become very attached to such a place. The driveway is splendid; the trees are in blossom. A little late in the season I think but the effect is wondrous; a tunnel of white and pink cherry blossom. When were the trees planted?

NTD: That was my father's great project. The drive had been flat before he started that and it was his mission to make his mark. I think each keeper of the Hall feels they must provide some sort of enhancement. The building itself has had very little done to it. Of course it has had to be re plumbed and rewired and I have had the interior of the kitchen completely replaced. Then there was the installation of the en-suite bathrooms to some of the guest rooms but the Hall, from the exterior, is essentially as it was when it was built. Somehow, I don't feel the new kitchen matches what my father did to the drive. There are certain times of the year when the drive is "wondrous", as you say.
BOW: I recall the lights on the trees as I left in December, it had just begun snowing for the first time that winter and there was that stillness you get when snow falls.

NTD: Yes, in winter, when it is dark, when it snows. And in spring with the blossom. And then again in autumn, when the leaves turn. It really does mark the seasons. That is exactly what my father intended. He was very passionate about that project. They used nearly 500 tonnes of topsoil to create the mounds (as I call them) and there are 500 cherry trees, 500 exactly, 250 on each side of the drive and not one of them was lost. The research he did was incredible; the types of trees the type of soil, the way and time of the year the trees were to be planted.

CHRONICLES OF THE BUILDING OF THE RIPPLESWADE WALL

NTD: It was my grandfather's great project to build a large stone wall around approx. 30 acres of the property from the frontage and around the Hall. Fredericke was obsessed by this wall – it was designed to have concrete foundations 6 foot in depth and the wall was to be 12 feet in height and nearly four foot thick. Fredericke was obsessed with keeping foxes out. He had three Persian cats, which were like children to him and he lived in fear that they would be taken by the foxes. There used to be a lot of foxes in this area. Fredericke arranged for prison gangs to be employed to build the wall and despite advises to the contrary he began the wall at the back of the property at the furthest point from the public highway. Nearly 2.5 miles of wall were built whilst Fredericke was alive but the work ceased almost immediately upon his passing.

The project took on Biblical significance. This was to be The Great Wall of Rippleswade Hall; a monument to Victorian industry and endeavour. A testament to dogged work and perseverance. It would keep out the rest of the world and Rippleswade Hall would be a sanctuary of peace and calm whilst the rest of the world went mad. Three hundred men worked on the project and two lost their lives. Over 2,000 cubic metres of foundations were dug and over 1,000 tonnes of masonry was erected. Once completed it would have been visible from near outer space. Construction began on 20 July 1921 and work continued on and off for the next 13 years. Because of its height and size the engineers had recommended that every 35 metres flying buttresses be used as support.

The two and a half miles of wall that stand today are hidden from public view and lie almost precisely in the middle of the Estate. It is a testament to the engineering, and typical of the over engineering of that time, that no part of it has cracked or broken and the only thing that has failed are the five wooden gateways (each large enough to allow a tractor through it) as the wooden gates have long since rotted. Fredericke had always intended that certain parts of the wall would have exotic climbers and plants that needed to be shielded from heavy winds and harsh frosts. Certain clematis have self seeded and the effect as the summer sun begins to fall is striking. The green verdant plants clambering on the gold stone as it reflects the fading warmth of the sun.

BOW: I assume your father is no longer with us. I mean to say he would still be here in residence …

NTD: You are correct. He passed away three years ago. Although he spent the last 17 months in a care home, he did not die here and there are times when that bothers me a great deal. He should have died here at his home and I see that now. But at the time it had become so difficult, he had been ill for many years and I had cared for him, along with a resident carer. It got to the stage when it just became too much. When he passed away it seemed like a blessing, it sounds awful but a great burden had been lifted. Do you know I didn't cry, not when he died and not at his funeral. It was only much later that I cried, and then only briefly.

BOW: My condolences, I think I grasp what you mean. I was also surprised by my reaction to my father's death. You have it exactly. It haunts us doesn't it? We were not terribly close but in our own funny sort of way we loved each other but more as reluctant friends than as family. We rubbed along as they say. I was never quite sure whether he was irritated or disappointed by me, or perhaps more cruelly was he just indifferent?

NTD: It is a curious thing isn't it? If anything my father was a little too ….well, after my mother's stroke he seemed to abandon her, and it were almost as if I became his ….I was only ….
[A short silence]

BOW: Yes, the begetters of life can be very odd. By the end I felt a distant indifference, nowhere near as strong as dislike, just indifference and I think he knew it. But I am not sure he really cared.

NTD: My relationship with my father bothers me greatly, it did then and it does now. It significantly impacted my life. It stifled me – in his own subtle way he was very controlling. In the end that is what did for my mother. I just could not feel any real grief and despite everything I believe that I should have. Now I am haunted by the circumstances of his death and the fact he did not die at Rippleswade Hall.

BOW: We had an adopted cat called El Pedro, I always called him El Pedro. His real name was Peter but who calls a cat Peter for God's sake? We had to have him put down nearly three years ago and my wife and I cried child-tears at the vet and on the way home. The next morning, I watched myself cry in front of the mirror when I was shaving. A silly old man crying over a cat. My grief surprised me and it took me some time to come to an understanding – I had unconditionally loved that cat. I think I was distraught when we had him put down, sounds dramatic I know, but I really think I was. Far more distraught than when my own father died and the only explanation I could come up with was because I gave love rather than received it. That's when it really hurts – when you lose those to whom you give love. Odd isn't it – grief is so different when it is for those that loved you – parents, grandparents, uncles and aunts. It is a grief consumed in selfishness and guilt – unspoken words echo in the memory like footsteps down a hallway that we should have walked to a door we should have opened …….

NTD: You are very wise Mr Whibley.

34

BOW: Sorry, my apologies I seem to have gotten a little side-tracked.

NTD: Not at all. What you just said was almost poetic. Do you like poetry?

BOW: Some, a little. I struggle with poetry, I think many of the poets struggle with poetry. Some time ago I read that Eliot had originally written *The Wasteland* and *The Hollow Men* as one poem and that it was Ezra Pound that had suggested they worked much better as two poems. *Il miglior fabbro* could not be truer. All the critical essays talking about the symphonic qualities of *The Wasteland* – it barely makes sense if you read *The Wasteland* and *The Hollow Men* together as one poem. I prefer a good piece of fiction. I find myself increasingly re reading old favourites.

NTD: Indeed.

BOW: My apologies, it is not right that I sit with you and pontificate on literature.

NTD: Not at all, I very much enjoyed our last meeting. You are clearly a well-read man. I would so like it for you to meet the local doctor and minister. They too enjoy similar discussions and I find myself a little alone these days.

BOW: Perhaps if we have time after my inspection we can take another coffee. We ran out of time on my last visit and I must ensure that I am not so tardy this time.

NTD: Of course, I see.

BOW: Perhaps we could go now to the three rooms I saw only briefly on my last visit. Would that be alright?

NTD: Yes of course.

BOW: Please lead the way, I don't think I can remember the way if my life depended on it.

NTD: Of course, let's hope it doesn't.

BOW: Indeed.

NTD: You must see the The Prayer Room, it is just here. Can you spare a few moments? It has always been called "The Prayer Room", not the Chapel or the Crypt.

BOW: Well time presses a little.

NTD: It is just that on Wednesday mornings we light the candles and incense. It was my father's idea, a time for quiet inward reflection – he came here often, particularly after my mother passed away. There should still be a pool of his tears.

BOW: Yes, let's see The Prayer Room, as you say, a few minutes will not hurt.

NTD: Here we are.

BOW: I see what you mean. Very impressive, very beautiful; like everything at Rippleswade Hall. Are those Tibetan prayer flags hanging on the wall?
NTD: Yes they are. I am impressed, how observant and knowledgeable of you! Have you been to Tibet?

BOW: No, I am afraid not.

[I need to say something about this visit to The Prayer Room. Something odd occurred. As we had stood looking up at the ornate ceiling, NTD had, in my view, deliberately and provocatively rubbed against me. She had gently rested her hand on my forearm and then she had squeezed past me, face to face, bosom to bosom, as it were. Not much I could do or say it happened very quickly].

[I probably ought to add that The Prayer Room was quite possibly the most beautiful and opulent "room" I have ever seen. Far more than a chapel, it was an exquisite homage to all of the main religions. An ornate crucifix sat upon a detailed carved oak table next to which sat a grey stone Buddha, smiling serenely in a meditative pose. Gold leaf icons were hung next to the prayer flags. Printed excerpts from the Koran and the Old Testament were framed and hung on the wall. What appeared to be a very large and illustrated family Bible lay open on a lectern. The small central dome was intricately tiled with gold tiles and there was a turquoise inlay. The walls were marble in part, some stone and some wood, beech I think. The floor was covered with light grey flag stones. There were numerous rugs upon it. There must have been hundreds of candles, all lit. To one side there was a large, very tall and green fig tree in a ceramic pot, which was shaped like a Middle Eastern minaret. There was the sound of running water, although not immediately obvious where this came from. There was a mixture of church pews, Quaker chairs and large very colourful cushions in rich plum, blues and ornate covers with tassels and ornate beadings. A number of wind chimes hung silently].

[Here the tape is left running for a while and movement can be heard but there is no dialogue].

BOW: (Slightly breathless) I had forgotten the stairs. That is the closest to a work out I have had for some time.

NTD: Mr Whibley, I am sorry I am so used to flitting around the Hall, I completely forget. Please, sit here for a minute and gather your breath. Can I get you some water?

BOW: You are most kind, no, no water thank you. Let me sit here for a few moments. Thank you.

NTD: It is two long flights of stairs to get to this floor. There was once talk of having a lift fitted but it would have been so very expensive and my grandfather loathed the idea of something so ugly and cumbersome in the heart of his beloved Hall.

BOW: I can well see that. Although one of those old Parisian lifts may have looked well opposite the grand staircase.

NTD: How odd, that was exactly my thought. But it never happened and it never will.

BOW: Never?

NTD: Even the most beautiful lift in the world would have offended my grandfather's vision.

BOW: Yes, I see.

NTD: Are you ready to continue, it is not far now?

BOW: Indeed, thank you. But if I may I would like to use a rest-room if I may.

NTD: Why of course, there is the only en suite on this floor in the bedroom suite just along the hall.

BOW: Ah, I will need a few minutes, to freshen up you see.

NTD: That is fine, just fine.
BOW: What I mean to say is …….

Toilet Etiquette

An addendum is required here as the dialogue alone seems a little odd and sometimes that which is not said needs explaining. Gentlemen, as they get older, begin to find changes in their habits and, parts of the anatomy begin to work differently. In the case in point for a man the sitting usage of the toilet becomes more eccentric and personal in nature. Firstly, as a general rule one prefers, where possible, not to be overheard and on this point the Japanese toilet culture has much to commend itself. In Japan, the use of music, often Abba I understand, is a popular way of dealing with this conundrum. Secondly, the activity leads to something much less savoury with regard to the olfactory system. A considerate host or hostess will always provide air freshener. Thirdly, the mission somehow becomes far messier and spread out than in earlier life. Or is it that we just did not notice this when we were younger? My father began creating a nest with toilet paper in the bowl before he used it, which with a judicious flush dealt with the issues in a most economic way, or at least it did for him. My own attempts at nest building had been far less successful, being literally blown and blasted away before completion of the emissions.

I was trying to politely convey to NTD that I would like a little privacy. I believe she had a sense of what I was clumsily trying to communicate but she was rather more focused on the practicalities of leaving me alone in this large house, myself having already emphasised on more than one occasion that I must make proper use of my time on this visit.

There is no need to go into too much further detail other than to note that I had to go through the excruciating humiliation of using the "can" whilst NTD waited in the adjoining room for me. No Abba, air freshener, or toilet brush!

BOW: Yes, err thank you for waiting. Let's press on. Well this is certainly a splendid property and surprisingly large inside. Not, of course, that it looks small from the outside, it is just that the interior is deceptively large and spacious. This hallway is very wide and the rooms are well appointed. How many rooms are there in Rippleswade Hall?

NTD: There are 33 rooms not including The Prayer Room, basement and outbuildings.

BOW: It looks well as my grandfather used to say, it looks well.

NTD: I am not sure I follow.

BOW: A turn of phrase, it means nothing really, but it sounds well. Hah. Just a silly way of saying things are good.

NTD; Ah, I see.

BOW: There are a lot of framed photographs, mainly black and white – your father?

NTD: Yes, his first and great passion, apart from the Hall, was photography, then he became hugely interested in processing and developing and then finally as he got older he loved mounting and framing the photographs. At the last count I got to 297! Some of them are very beautiful, I sometimes wonder whether I shouldn't sponsor an exhibition.

BOW: What a fine idea. Is that Bali?

NTD: No it isn't, how curious, so many people say that about this photograph. It was taken in the Buri Gandaki river gorge in Nepal, one of my father's favourite places in the world. He took me there when I was sixteen, it was simply magical and I understood my father so much better after going on that trip with him. He was one of the few westerners who did not need a guide, something of which he was very proud. He was not a climber as such, but a keen walker/trekker. He so loved that valley and having been there with him I can understand why. I have never been back.

BOW: Quite beautiful, the setting, the photograph and the photography. Perhaps it would have been even better if you had been in it.

NTD: (In a serious tone) No, no, he took too many photos of ....for a while, as a teenager, I shared his passion for photography but once the digital era came in all the magic vanished for me. Somehow, it changed everything, for me at least, although not for my father. For a while it made him cling on even tighter. We would spend hours in the dark room when he came back from his expeditions. It were almost as though we were unwrapping exotic parcels as the negatives were developed. It was an isolated existence here at Rippleswade Hall, particularly for a teenage girl, so perhaps I did not see the signs, does one ever in those circumstances? There, I have said a little too much...

BOW: Yes, well err.

NTD: Here, you see this photo is somewhere in Bali but no one ever gets that. I sometimes wonder if the photos got mixed up but I checked and my father checked – he was an assiduous cataloguer as well. Definitely no mistake, I have been there and the other photo is Nepal. My father's passions were trekking, photography and sailing and my mother shared none of them. For awhile.my father got me involved in sailing. He so wanted me to sail in the Olympics, but that was his dream. My father went on many expeditions, as he called them, on his own, or perhaps more accurately without my mother. It is only now, so many years later that that strikes me as a little odd. It is curious isn't it, that as children and young adults we are not particularly questioning of our parents. I certainly wasn't. Father went off, sometimes for months and mother stayed at home.

BOW: Yes, I think that starts when you have your own children.
NTD: As I think you are aware, I have no children and the rest of my family reside in the US or the Caribbean. They have all made it clear they have no intention of relocating back here to take over and manage Rippleswade Hall when I have passed away. My father and grandfather would be so disappointed. This was meant to be a family legacy that passed down generation to generation through hundreds of years. The Trust will ensure the Hall is fully maintained, but what

is the point if no one is actually living here? It makes me so sad. I deeply feel the failure, Mr Whibley. The responsibility and my failure weighs heavily on me. So we are nearly there, just a few doors along.

BOW: At last, that felt like a hard workout, for me at least.

NTD: (Laughing) Really Mr Whibley, we shall have to get you into shape.

BOW: Yes I would like that. What I mean to say is I have been meaning for some time to take up some moderate exercise.

NTD: Well day to day life at Rippleswade Hall constantly does that for me. There is no shortage of stair work. Do you know I was once stopped by an older man at a railway station in Vietnam and he asked if I was from Holland. Why do you think he asked that? It was because of my beautiful, firm and shapely bottom he said – he said ladies in Holland do a lot of cycling and it does wonders for their bottoms. Flattering as that might be, I was only 17 or 18 at the time and I never wore those trousers again – funny the things that stay with you. At the time I was not at all pleased, but it became a story my father was fond of recounting and I suppose there is an odd, funny side to it. My father kept teasing me that I really should wear those trousers again, usually just as we were getting ready to go out, or when he was practising with a new lens for his camera. So here we are. This is the room where the fire started and it is the adjoining rooms on either side that were also affected and also this portion of the hallway. Shall I give you a while to make your investigations and return in say 30 minutes or an hour? I have no idea about these things.

BOW: Oh, I should think that 30 minutes will be more than ample. I really just need to take some more photographs and take some measurements. Yes, if you could pop back at say 10:45 – would that be alright?

NTD: Absolutely, there are a number of things I need to get done this morning, so if you don't mind I will leave you to it.

This is where the recording ends, although it is clearly not the end of my visit. As discussed with NTD, I spent approx. 30 minutes taking photographs, measurements and notes in the three rooms. The seat of the fire was not as I expected to find it. The preliminary theory that it had been an electrical fault seemed difficult to substantiate. The severe fire damage was not inside the plug socket as one would expect to find but rather was on the outside of the plug socket. The pattern of fire damage led me to believe that some sort of incendiary fluid had been poured onto the plug socket surface and then lit. It was clear that there was no plug in the plug socket at the time of the fire. If the fire began inside the plug socket, as it can occasionally, the ignition and spread is from the inside outwards, so the inside of the socket is more badly burnt than the outside. If the fire began in the plug of an electrical device then again the pattern of fire is different. This immediately created an awkward situation. I found it hard to believe that NTD was the perpetrator of a fraudulent insurance claim but the evidence strongly pointed towards misadventure. In my experience the best thing to do is explain the concerns and see how the insured reacts and if they can provide any sort of explanation. I began to feel lightheaded as I contemplated how to best tackle this with NTD.

NTD did not return by 10:45 as we had agreed, and after approx. ten minutes I decided to try and make my way to the kitchen/lobby, which seemed to be the hub of Rippleswade Hall. That old cat killer got the better of me and I opened one of the doors on the opposite side of the hallway from the rooms where the fire had been. Upon opening the door I was extremely surprised to see what appeared to be a very elderly person. It was not possible to discern whether it was a man or a woman, lying on his/her side on a small single bed. They were covered by a sheet and blanket, which was excessively neatly placed over them. The person was facing the door and the curtains were drawn in the room, so the room was in semi darkness. On a chair, on the opposite side of the bed, was a small Asian lady, I would guess Filipino, who simply and very slowly motioned by raising her index finger to her lips that I should not speak or make any noise. I stood motionless by the door, neither taking a few steps further into the room, or a step back, so I just stood there for a few moments staring. The eyes of the "patient" were open extremely widely as if they had witnessed something truly horrifying. So wide that it were as if their soul had been touched by darkness. Upon retreating and quietly shutting the door, it immediately struck me that this chance discovery created a further difficulty for me, as it was a fact that ordinarily I would need to include in my report. What if this elderly person was a smoker, a convicted arsonist (likely far-fetched) or a psychotic? And what about the "nurse"? To say nothing in my report would be unprofessional and so now I had two delicate issues that I needed to discuss with NTD. In the accident report form completed by NTD she had stated she was the sole resident at Rippleswade Hall.

After closing the door and taking only a few steps down the hall, NTD appeared. She immediately apologised explaining that she had been on the phone with her accountant. I tried to reassure her that it was quite alright but perhaps I was not as convincing as I might have been. I believe NTD sensed my displeasure, irritation even, and immediately suggested a coffee. As we walked down to the kitchen I realised that this was not the right time to talk about the possible arson claim, nor about the "patient". By the time we had reached the kitchen the mood had lightened, at least on my part and we made polite conversation for about 20 minutes or so. I noticed as I got into my car that it was precisely 11:30 a.m.

Shown to me now and marked "**BOW 4** " is my report on the fire.

The above is a detailed and accurate account of my second visit to Rippleswade Hall.

Somewhere between our first meeting and the end of the second meeting I fell in love with NTD. There, I have said it and it is now a matter of public record. NTD was, still is for that matter, very beautiful and has a sort of quiet self-confidence that is neither arrogant nor condescending. I would go so far as to say she is a beautiful person, living in a truly resplendent property and for whom life has been just a little less difficult than for most of us. But she knows that and somehow acknowledges it. I am an overweight middle aged man to whom love should not come so easily. The semen is dulled, much weaker now and the hormones have faded. The passion of youth has lost its raging intensity. Of course it is different falling in love at my age – completely different to the volcanic lust I once felt. But it is still a wonderful feeling, an all-consuming experience, like a sweet fever that both plagues you and fascinates you in equal measure. For clarification I am bound to say that I am very happily married and to be absolutely clear these were not feelings I had any intention of acting upon.

Ode to Nathalie

She was serene, like tranquillity
She was still, like calmness
She was radiant, like fire
She was love, like red hot
She was beauty, like stunning
She was exquisite, like diamonds

My report into the fire at Rippleswade Hall was completed one week after this second visit. Perhaps it was because I was dealing with such a beautiful lady and perhaps because Rippleswade Hall was so impressive but I felt that an outright allegation of fraud somehow blighted both NTD and the Hall. In short, I could not bring myself to be totally frank and honest in my report, something I have prided myself on in my professional career. My report concluded that the cause of the fire was inconclusive and indeterminate and that absent other/further evidence the claim needed to be adjusted and settled.

In 2009, insurers uncovered 130,000 fraudulent claims worth £1.32 billion across all insurance products.

Insurers invest at least £200 million each year to identify fraud.

Normally, I would have gone onto adjust the quantum of the claim but nothing further was ever referred to me, which would suggest that some sort of deal was done between Gluckman and NTD but about which I have no knowledge. It is with great shame that I must confess that my professional judgment was severely clouded but what I will say is that this is the only time this has happened in my professional career.

64.   The Dinner

65.   I was very surprised to receive a formal dinner invitation from NTD. It arrived by first class post and was posted in an expensive envelope on which my name and address were set out in immaculate handwritten black ink. Indeed, it was so immaculate I thought that the envelope with the address had been printed. Shown to me now and marked "**BOW 5** " is a copy of the invitation. The invitation was on a gold trimmed card and requested the pleasure of the company of Barrington Olivier Whibley for dinner at 7:00 p.m. Thursday 21 June.

66.   There were a number of things that struck me as odd. Firstly, she had used my full name and must have done research to discover that my middle name is Olivier. Secondly, she had not invited my wife Joanne as well, which I have to agree with my wife was odd. Thirdly, the invitation was received exactly two months before the actual event (thought that sort of notice was only for weddings and significant parties). Fourthly, was the fact of the invitation at all. I had only met the woman twice before and spoken on the telephone on a few other occasions and always this had been to do with my appointment as a loss adjuster investigating the fire damage claim on behalf of her insurance company. My immediate thought was that this must be the dinner whereby I was to be introduced to the local doctor and vicar whom she had mentioned on my second visit. There was nothing in the invitation to indicate this would be the case but I simply assumed it was.

67.   I have to confess being in somewhat of a quandary as to how to reply. I do not mean whether I accepted or not, it was too interesting an invitation to turn down. What I mean was, how was I to respond? It felt like an invitation from Buckingham Palace, what do you say, to whom, how? In the end I typed a short letter gratefully accepting the invitation; there was almost no need to put the date in my diary as I became rather consumed by the event.

68.   The picture I had in my mind's eye was a dinner with four of us in the kitchen, with NTD sat next to me and on the other side of the

table the older doctor and vicar. I quietly fantasised that for one evening only I would act as her partner.

69. An unusual amount of time was spent preparing for the dinner party and even Joanne became involved in assisting with my wardrobe. Indeed, it was Joanne who suggested I treat myself to a light-weight suit, something I had talked about acquiring for some time, but as my wife said with my rather portly figure a lightweight khaki coloured suit just added pounds to me. In the end I did buy a pair of new dark grey trousers and a rather fine boating blazer that we found in a local gentleman's tailor. I would have to say that with a crisply ironed white shirt, no tie and well polished black brogues I rather felt the part.

70. It seemed important to me that the time of my arrival should be just right. Certainly not early but a polite 15 minutes after the scheduled time on the invitation. I did not wish to seem too eager and my wife suggested that I arrive a full 30 minutes late but after giving the matter careful consideration I decided 20 minutes had just the right tone. Not too early so as to seem too keen but not too late so as to appear casual. I definitely did want NTD to know that I was flattered by the invitation.

71. It had not been wasted on me that the date for the dinner was the summer solstice; my grandfather's birthday and I have always toasted Grandpa Fred's birthday even though he passed away over 30 years ago. Could I, should I raise a glass during the dinner and ask NTD to join me in honouring a man that had had such an important part in my life, or did I do it silently at some stage without making any comment?

72. The 21 June was a glorious day, there were clear blue skies and I had deliberately kept the day free so I could savour getting ready slowly. But it was the sort of day that beckons you outside. There was a gentle warming breeze and the lawn needed mowing, the two front borders needed to be weeded. It had been a wet spring and the warm sunshine of the preceding week had sent nature into a frenzied

growing spell. Time had also been set aside so that I could go to our nearest wine merchant who could advise on a crisp bottle of chardonnay to be a contribution to what I suspected would be a glorious feast. A trip to Richard's wine shop always took at least 90 minutes as he was a great raconteur and I rather liked the idea of telling him in some detail what and to who the wine was to be given. I just knew he would be a tiny bit jealous and that added just a little more frisson to what was already a rather exquisite day.

73.   But the best laid plans etc …The gardening ended up taking far longer than I had wanted it to, not least the fact that I had not reckoned on spending some time with my neighbour Jon who was having trouble with his mower and upon hearing me using mine popped over and we then had a long chat about plans for summer holidays. All of a sudden it was 15:00 and I knew that I would need to leave at 17:30 if my carefully timed plan was to work. The wine buying and chat with Richard was going to have to be fore shortened.

74.   With no little anxiety I was ready to leave at 17:15 but it had been far more hurried that I had imagined and Richard was not at the wine shop – he had an afternoon off, golfing and his wife had assisted me and I had rather badly explained my dinner invitation to her. It had come out all wrong without any of the delicious subtle suggestions I had delighted in imagining going through with Richard. In truth, I find his wife a little intimidating. She knew as much, if not more, about wine than Richard and she has an extremely posh accent that immediately makes you feel like you are one of the staff. She was one of the few women I can think of that I know who I would call handsome. She was most certainly not beautiful, nor was she ugly. She had straggly blonde hair, striking blue eyes and always wore a cotton blouse with an upturned collar. Her make up was surprisingly badly applied and she had a poor complexion. On close inspection, she had a Roman nose, which gave her a striking profile. She was not a woman many men would have flirted with. Joanne had once described her as "frightening" and that had rather taken me aback but it made sense. Camilla had a very direct look and always listened

very carefully to what you were saying. Richard has an immediate rapport with people and Camilla does not. In fact, although I had known her for some 15 years, I still felt we were simply acquaintances. She recommended a Cotes de Rhone, an unusual choice I thought, but she was very confident that on a warm summer's night this would be an ideal partner with fish, chicken and salad.

75. Presumptuously, I had it in mind that whatever wine I took would be used during dinner and it was only as I drove to Rippleswade Hall that I recalled that with the exquisite wine cellar NTD kept so well stocked, my offering was more than likely to remain unopened. The day had not changed and it was a glorious evening. During the drive there I imagined the doctor and vicar. Although never met or seen by me before I had a curiously acute impression of how each man would look.

76. The Cherry tree drive up to Rippleswade Hall on that summers evening was simply glorious. The sunlight danced on the leaves and, whilst shaded, the warmth of the evening sun could still be felt. There was a quality about the light; there is a Scott's artist called David Mackie whose paintings dwell on the way in which sunlight moves through and bounces onto trees. The drive up to Rippleswade Hall that evening is the closest I have ever felt to being in a painting.

77. As planned, I arrived at precisely 19:20 and was a little surprised there were no other cars outside, although I immediately thought to myself that on such a glorious evening a few drinks would mean that someone local could simply call for a cab. I parked near the front entrance and then rang the bell although the front door was wide open. I was a little taken aback when a reasonably elderly man with a walking stick moved slowly toward the front door. By my estimation he would have been in his late seventies. He was bald and had silver hair that was not well cut and some of which had been grown to comb over his bald patch. He appeared to have suffered from a stroke as his left leg and arm seemed to be largely immobile.

He walked with a slight stoop and he smiled faintly as he approached and just said "Mr Whibley" in a very soft but clear manner. He then turned slowly and indicated that I should follow him. I think I commented that it was a beautiful evening and decided that I would give the wine to NTD, so kept hold of the bottle that was now only slightly chilled.

78.   We moved slowly towards the kitchen and I walked a few paces behind. There was no-one in the kitchen, and I noted there were a number of pans and items in the process of preparation. The door to the herb garden was open and I realised that the man was going to take me somewhere outside. It was only after we had walked through the walled herb garden and through a large black iron gateway that I saw NTD seated at a table on the lawn beyond the herb garden and near the large oak tree. There were four large burners forming a square around the table and the setting looked wonderful. NTD rose and greeted me with a wave and at that point the man stepped aside to let me pass. He bowed his head ever so slightly and then turned slowly to return to the kitchen. On reflection, in my keenness to see NTD I did not say anything else to him.

79.   By the time I got to the table NTD was seated again and I approached with perhaps a little more haste than I would have wished to show and pressed the wine into her hands with a comment that it was a very small offering. She had gotten up again to greet me with a kiss to the cheek. In fact the wine had cost £38 and was more than I had spent on any bottle of alcohol, save for a bottle of champagne for a wedding anniversary. NTD did me the courtesy of looking at the wine and said that would be just fine with the main course. She immediately seemed different to the two previous occasions when we had met. She was wearing some subtle make up, which she had not done before and this accentuated her eyes and lips. She was wearing a loose white robe and a gold necklace and diamond earrings. Her hair was loose and tousled, as though she had just arrived at the table from her bed. Near her seat was a silver wine holder and stand in which there was an already opened bottle of

champagne. The sun caught the filigree on the stand and holder and it glinted at me. NTD noticed and smiled.

80.   She retook her seat and beckoned for me to sit as well and it was only then that I noticed the table had been set for two. The table was rectangular in shape and in the middle of it was a large ornate silver platter and on a mountain of ice were a couple of dozen oysters. The way the oysters had been arranged in the ice made them look like the rice fields in Bali and I commented on that. Her lips parted and curled and speaking a little more loudly and quickly than I had been previously heard her speak of she said "Exactly, you have it exactly, I knew you would."

81.   Some of the oysters had already been opened and were sitting in one half of their shell whilst others were still whole. There was a condiment platter near the tray on which there was silver salt and pepper shakers, a bottle of Tabasco, a small bottle of Lee & Perrins and a China bowl with lemons cut into wedges and each neatly wrapped in gauze. I have never heard of Tabasco or Worcester sauce being decanted but the setting seemed to almost suggest that it should be. The bottles seemed out of place on the silver tray amongst the fine china and glistening crystal. But then I think that I am being pedantic. Directly in front of me were three plates each of a different size stacked on top of each other and exquisite silver cutlery, perfectly polished. There were three crystal wine glasses as well as a champagne flute to my right hand and a white napkin rolled into a silver holder on top of the plate.

82.   I was only just starting to take things in around me and NTD said effusively that Peter had done such a good job in laying the table and getting everything ready. Cautiously, I said that I assumed Peter was the butler who had met me at the front door and he did not seem to be in good health. I have no idea why I said that, not even today having been able to give the point much thought, and perhaps it was NTD's reaction that made me realise that this was an odd comment/observation. She said, "In what way?" I said, "He's over

seventy, apparently the victim of a bad stroke, he is under weight and has a slight jaundiced look about him." NTD said "Some are more fortunate than others," But I just cannot recall if she said, "Some of us" or just "Some". To my mind that is important. She said, "There is nothing to be done, let it go." but it were as if she were talking to someone else, I had the strong feeling she was not talking to me when she said that.

83. NTD said that she hoped that I liked oysters and it must have been the look on my face because as she got up to serve me champagne she again smiled very broadly and said, "Enjoying eating oysters is very similar to enjoying a clitoris, they look and taste similar and I adore oysters. You are clearly not a man who likes oral sex". Blushing far more than I ought, I fidgeted in my chair and knocked over the champagne flute, which broke at the stem as it fell on the condiment tray. Having just been filled, the champagne now made a wet puddle on the crisp white tablecloth. NTD did not seem to notice at all, or if she did, did brilliantly pretending nothing had happened.

84. She again ran her left hand through her hair and in her right hand she poured out the champagne into a spare glass that seemed to miraculously appear from no-where. She was standing close beside me and my hand was on the chair arm and her thigh gently rubbed against it, I am not sure if she noticed but I did. With her left hand she gently touched my shoulder. Leaving the bottle on the table near me she moved slowly back to her chair.

85. It hardly needs to be said that I was extremely taken aback and shocked by her comment. Having arrived expecting some intellectual debate with the local vicar and doctor this was so far away from what I had imagined or been expecting that I felt my recovery was rather good under the circumstances. I said, "I have tried oysters on many occasions and feel they are somewhat overrated, personally I prefer muscles, scallops and razor clams as they have a better taste and are better suited to being cooked in a

sauce. The reason why you can taste the sea when you eat an oyster is because the oysters still contain sea water."

86.   As I finished speaking I began to realise that NTD was very drunk and possibly also high. Her head was lolling back so that she could almost see the Oak tree directly behind her and then she slowly leant forward running her left hand through her hair again as she shook it out and said, "Well I hope you like Krug champagne, it is in my opinion superior to Crystal and Laurent-Perrier, do you not think?"

87.   I needed no further invitation to embark on a mini monologue on the subject of champagne. It took us immediately away from a sort of awkwardness and also diverted away from the broken flute that I had laid on the left-hand corner of the table next to me. NTD had left the champagne on the table and I poured myself a generous refill.

88.   NTD began to eat an opened oyster. She liberally smothered it with Worcester sauce, Tabasco and pepper and just before she poured the contents of the shell into her mouth she laughed and said, "No need for salt. I like it that you mentioned Bali. Do you know I love Indonesia, the food, the people the climate. Have you ever been to Indonesia?" Again, I felt embarrassed that I had not, NTD seemed so worldly and made me feel so drab and suburban.

89.   Music began to play from somewhere within the Hall and as we were no more than 20 metres or so away from some of the opened windows it was clearly audible. What surprised me was that it was one of my favourite pieces of classical music and the only piece of music that I can say with certainty that I would like played at my funeral. It was the second movement of Philip Glass's violin concerto, which begins very softly. Perhaps what light breeze there was that night blew the hypnotic piece just that bit closer to us. I have heard the piece many hundreds, perhaps even thousands of times, but I never tire of listening to it. Without either of us needing to say anything we both sat and listened. Just as the recording moved into the third movement Peter appeared from the kitchen door and

began to move slowly towards us trying to carry what looked like an earthen pot – what I later realised was the pasta course. It was only then that I saw there was a printed menu on a small silver card-holder sitting near the oyster tray. The menu read as follows:

Dublin Bay oysters
(Krug 1985)
Rabbit, wilde mushroom, truffle and Madeira sauce with pasta tortellini
(Chateau Neuf de Pape 1969)
Turbot (merniere) with baby asparagus and creamed spinach
(Puilly fume Grand Cloche 1997)
Cloud berries and Chantilly cream
(Constantia Cape Blessed 1983)
Du fromage
(Quinta Do Noval 1992)

90.   NTD watched me read the menu with the self-confidence she did not need to justify anything. Du fromage. There was a story and I knew I had to tell it. I explained to NTD that many years ago I had taken my wife to Paris – it had been one of our first trips abroad. It was in the days when James Bond being in Jamaica was amazingly exciting – only millionaires and royalty went to the Caribbean – it was in the days when a long weekend at a cosy B&B in Bridlington was regarded as extravagant. Anyway, we went to Paris when it felt very exotic to do so, and for the first time I got to try out my school-boy French, in France. The Parisians, to a man were so rude – they pretended they could not understand any of my French. We had a rotten three days – every waiter, every shop keeper, every museum and gallery attendant were without fail unpleasant and surly.

91.   On the last night we went to a restaurant to have a modest fixed price menu – the food was delicious and we were the only foreigners, everyone else was Parisian and we were completely ignored. When it came to ordering the desserts we decided to share some cheese so when the waiter came to take the order I said in my best accent, "Du

54

fromage s'il vous plait." The waiter looked at me "Que?". I repeated, "Fromage s'il vous plait." The waiter said nothing but by his expression it was clear he did not understand what it was I was trying to say so I pointed to the menu "fromage" – ah "fromarjay". I couldn't help it I yelled out, "You French wanker, you know exactly what I meant." and the whole restaurant stopped and stared at us. "Du fromage" indeed. NTD laughed politely but it is a good story and warranted more than a polite laugh. That was the moment when the term "sniffy" first struck me as perhaps being just a little appropriate for NTD. It was the first time I had thought anything negative about her. She did not laugh in an appropriate manner at my funny story. But in her defence she was intoxicated and in my estimation, high/stoned or wired.

92.   I began to get up with the intention of helping Peter who was making poor progress and it seemed likely he would not get to the table with the rabbit dish still in its bowl. But as soon as I had made the smallest movement to get up, NTD beckoned with her hand that I should stay seated. I had not realised that she had been watching me through her tousled hair. She was crouching rather than sitting in her chair. Her feet were tucked under her knees on the chair and her hands were wrapped around her lower leg almost as though she were cold but it was still a warm evening and she seemed to be rocking ever so gently backwards and forwards. Her dress had fallen down her legs and her legs were both tanned and toned and the only other thing I can recall was she was bare footed. Perhaps I noticed a little too well as when she saw my gaze she adjusted her dress.

93.   Peter eventually made it to the table but by the time he arrived he looked very pale. He had developed a significant sweat and he was unable to place the bowl down quietly, the noise of it landing heavily onto the table seemed to awaken NTD out of her trance. NTD immediately asked if I minded helping her assist Peter "back to the house" as she put it. Of course I did not mind but I pointed out that the now panting Peter should perhaps sit for a little while to gather himself. Peter protested very feebly that he was fine and would sit

down when he got inside. It was clear he was not alright. What he seemed to need more than anything was water but that was the one thing not on the table so I took a fist full of the now melting ice from around the oysters and wrapped my serviette around it and NTD then began to dab this on Peter's forehead. He was now sitting in my chair and looked a little more composed. Upon seeing him at close quarters he looked even older than I had first estimated; I would have said that he must be at least seventy five – perhaps older. As his breathing regulated and some colour began to return to his face NTD in a very composed manner said she would call for the doctor and bring out a pitcher of water. I expected her to pull a mobile phone from somewhere but instead she walked in that languid gate she had toward the kitchen.

94.   Peter began to apologise, saying that NTD had made such an effort to make this work. He said, "I am zo zorry, zo zorry" and it was only then that I realised that English was not his first language. In an attempt to engage with him I asked where he was from and he seemed puzzled by that, he said, "I am from Rippleswade Hall. I have worked here for over 46 years; it has been my great honour to serve Ms. Merchitta and her family." It was my turn to be puzzled, it took a few moments to register that Ms. Merchitta was NTD. Why had he used that name?

95.   NTD had disappeared into the Hall and I was left standing beside an elderly butler who seemed a few minutes ago to be about to expire. My hostess seemed to be more or less off her face but was somehow holding it together and I was about to have one of the best meals of my life. I could not very well leave Peter and he seemed a little calmed, although still breathless and if anything becoming paler again. Having never met the man before, I had no way of knowing if he was simply pale of complexion. It was only then, as I stood there, that I realised I had my mobile in my jacket pocket but it was of no real use with NTD somewhere indoors phoning the local doctor and it did not occur to me that I should do anything else but wait for NTD to return, presumably with news of what it was she proposed we do next.

96. I cannot recall the following events in exactly the order in which they occurred but I do not see that anything crucial hangs on the precise order of events. What I can say is that I am clear that all of these facts occurred as I recount them now. **Fact 1** – at some stage whilst it was still light I looked at the Oak tree and I am quite clear that I saw a noose swaying in the breeze from one of the lower limbs of the tree. I am quite certain it was a noose. I saw it. I am absolutely clear about that and can see no reason for making this up. It was only much later in the evening that I became aware that it had been removed. When I saw the noose I was on my own and could not therefore have commented about it to anyone, which I certainly would have if anyone had been there. As I said the sequence of some of the events are hazy but that is all. It is possible that Peter was still sitting in my chair when I saw the noose but he was in no state to discuss anything – certainly not a noose. **Fact 2** – Peter began to deteriorate quite quickly. He became paler and his breathing became shallower and he began to perspire heavily. I began to feel more panicked. There was no sign of NTD and my first aid experience was limited to say the least. I recalled an email received through work many years ago, originally sent out by some charity in the US, in which they had advised that if someone has just had or appears to be about to have a heart attack that they should try and cough as hard as they can. I think there was also something about breathing in through the nose but what I did do was to tell Peter that he must try and cough as hard as he could. I think I did say that I thought he was about to have a heart attack and that this was best medical advice. It was not clear that Peter could hear me as by now he was slumped in the chair and his eyes were half closed. I began shouting into his ear that he should try and cough and he did make a couple of spluttering noises, which gave me the impression he was trying to do as I was advising him. Whether or not it was the correct thing to do I still do not know but I began to flick the ice-cold water from the oyster tray onto his forehead. By dipping my hand into the bottom of the oyster tray I was able to try and cool Peter's forehead. Peter looked far from comfortable in the chair and I decided he needed to lie flat. I manhandled Peter onto the ground and the grass was beginning to

show the very early signs of dew. By now I was beginning to feel quite agitated and having been on hypertension medication for over a decade I recognised the signs that my blood pressure had risen sharply. I became flushed and slightly breathless and my heart rate had risen as well. Maybe it was a panic attack but the clear thought flashed across my brilliant mind that by the time NTD returned there would be two of us out cold on the grass by the table. **Fact 3** – No matter what my physical state or the highly unusual circumstances, on the following point I have never been clearer in my life. Sitting, or more accurately squatting on the branch to which the noose was slung I saw The Devil, Satan, whatever you want to call him. Half human, half reptile I have never seen anything like that before or since, not in horror films, books, scientific journals, nature programmes. The Devil was no more than four-foot-tall with a dark grey gun mettle "skin". I say "skin" because I cannot properly say what it was, half reptile half animal, they were not scales but nor was it like human skin, there was no hair. His backbone was ridged. But the most striking thing was the pinkness around the edge of his mouth and the rims of his eyes, where the grey skin stopped. He had very red, blood shot eyes. He turned very slowly, looked me in the eye, pushed his lip to the front of his mouth, and that was it. He did not say anything, make any gesture, it was clear he saw me and I saw him for a few seconds only. I did not see from where he came or to where he went. I am adamant that what I saw was real and I knew instantly, without any hesitation, that that creature, figure, call him what you will, was Satan. My advisers have already been very clear as to their own thoughts on this particular part of my witness statement but I am bound to tell the truth, I understand that I must testify to its truthfulness so I cannot leave this out.

97.   For obvious reasons I was incredibly relieved to see NTD finally appear and somehow it was even more comforting that she was being followed by a man carrying what I now know to be a medical bag. There is a clarity about the following events that I am unable to explain. The man was tall and had a slim build, he was almost underweight, he had silver hair that was unruly but not un-kept;

almost as if it had not changed since he were at boarding school. He was wearing gold framed glasses and walked briskly with a broad stride. He was very upright from which I assumed him to be ex-military. He had on light brown chords, brown brogues and a blue cotton shirt with sleeves rolled up to the elbow. He was tanned and had a pleasant demeanour. When discussing him during my last visit, NTD had commented on what she had described as an unusual "facial gait", I think she meant facial expression but I saw none of that in this man. He was pleasant, calm and authoritative, exactly what was required. I felt myself calming quickly, my own breathing loosened and my tension began to slacken.

98.   As the doctor knelt to attend to Peter I noticed that he must have moved onto his side, I had laid him on his back and the first thing the doctor said was, "Good, good, thank God he is not on his back."

99.   It was only then that I realised I was clutching a small handful of ice in my right hand and as NTD noticed this I dropped the ice to the ground. It wasn't a gun! NTD did not immediately introduce us, perhaps for obvious reasons and Dr Chapman, as I later learnt his name was, had begun attending to Peter. NTD was very concerned and asked if she could do anything. Dr Chapman said not right away. He opened his bag and took out a stethoscope and listened to Peter's heart first from the back and then from the front, he then appeared to take his pulse. Peter appeared to be slipping in and out of consciousness and Dr Chapman began to administer CPR. He was extremely composed and calm and whilst he was pressing down on Peter's chest he said to NTD "We need an ambulance."

100.   I had taken my mobile phone out of my jacket pocket and keen that NTD did not disappear back into the Hall I dialled 999 from the mobile. NTD had not said a word to me since returning with the doctor and as I made the call Dr Chapman began trying to speak with Peter asking if he could hear him at all. Having explained that we needed the ambulance service I passed the phone to NTD who gave the operator the address and some directions and she in turn passed

the phone to Dr Chapman who explained that the patient was a 69 year old male, in poor health and he then mentioned some medical terms that I did not understand and cannot recall. He did say that the patient had suffered a suspected pulmonary embolism and urgently needed emergency hospital treatment. He explained that he was a GP and that Peter was one of his patients and that he would stay with him until the ambulance arrived.

101.   As he handed the mobile back to me he nodded his appreciation and said, "Andrew Chapman." and put out his hand. NTD apologised and said "I am so sorry, I have been rather thrown by all of this." and she waived her hands around the general area. "Not at all." I responded, "perfectly understandable in the circumstances." Then turning to Andrew I asked, "How is Peter?" "Not good I am afraid. He has had a serious heart attack, and we need to get him to hospital as soon as we can."

102.   It is difficult to be precise with time estimates, whilst my recollection of the events is clear, the period over which the events occurred seems unreal. NTD had begun to walk back towards the house explaining to Dr Chapman that she would need to direct the ambulance around to the back of the Hall. For some reason I followed her in and had sat myself down at the kitchen table. On the table was a sort of scrapbook and mainly for distraction I had begun reading the news paper cuttings stuck into the scrapbook. NTD disappeared, again – she may have said something as to where she was going or what she was doing, but I do not recall it.

103.   It seemed to take an age for the ambulance to arrive at Rippleswade Hall. NTD had disappeared and Andrew was busy attending to Peter and for some time I sat in the kitchen before going back outside. Andrew kept taking Peter's pulse and at one stage he began rummaging in his bag. He said, "Damn." and a little later "Ah good, very good." Andrew then took out a syringe and administered an injection into Peter's left arm. It was very tempting to ask Andrew what he was doing but under the circumstances it just did not seem

appropriate and Andrew seemed pre-occupied. NTD had taken my mobile, inadvertently I am sure and as I stood near the table it struck me that there was some wonderful food going to waste.

104. The one significant point is that I clearly noticed the noose had disappeared and I waddled over to more closely inspect the branch onto which I had seen it attached and upon which Satan had been crouching. The scene was unremarkable, there were no signs or damage on the limb, there was nothing on the grass underneath the branch and there was nothing on the trunk of the tree. It was mystifying but the noose was very clearly not there now.

105. I would describe myself as reasonably self aware and it was clear to me that I felt far from normal at that stage of the evening. At first I attributed this to the wine, to the excitement and euphoria of the occasion, to the company of NTD, to the events with Peter, to seeing the noose and then Satan. It was the sum of all of these things but it was something else as well. My head just did not feel right, did not feel normal.

106. Finally, NTD came striding very purposefully from behind the Oak tree. Behind her, and making slow progress over the thick turf was an ambulance that still had its blue lights flashing, which seemed both unnecessary and odd. The ambulance stopped approx. 30 yards on the other side of the Oak tree and the two paramedics got out with some bags and began to run after NTD.

107. Andrew seemed particularly relieved to see them and began to explain his diagnosis and what he had done. One of the paramedics ran back to the ambulance and began to get the stretcher out of the back of the ambulance. NTD was standing a little away from me and she still held my mobile in her hand. I moved over to stand next to her and gently retrieved my phone. Without warning this gave me a real sense of relief as though deep down this is what had been agitating me.

108. It seems curious to say it now, but one of the paramedics seemed to me to be clearly Down's Syndrome. Surely someone with Down's Syndrome cannot be a paramedic? It just seemed extraordinary. On reflection, and with the wisdom of much hard thought and hindsight it seems likely that this was when the hallucinations began to start, or was it when I saw the swinging noose and Satan crouched above it? [Have I mentioned the noose was swinging?] The significance of the timing of this is that if I was drugged it must have been either in the champagne or the oysters as these were the only things I had eaten/drunk since arriving. At that given time it was my clear view that one of the paramedics was severely Down's Syndrome and should not have been attending anybody in that capacity. Perhaps I should have said something, but as Andrew seemed non-plussed it seemed best to leave things to the experts.

109. The three medical people had carefully gotten Peter onto the stretcher and were wheeling him slowly back to the ambulance with Andrew walking behind holding his bag. Instinctively, both NTD and myself followed as well. Truthfully, we straggled behind, uncertain as to what we should do next. To my surprise we were gently holding hands. For a few moments of my life I was Lord Rippleswade and the strange thing was I was hard as a rock.

110. NTD asked Andrew, "Is there anything we can do? Shall I follow you in the car?" Andrew was quite emphatic. "No, there is nothing you can do, it is probably best to stay here. I will go with Peter in the ambulance and call you when there is news."

111. It took some time for me to begin to calm down and I recall realising that dusk was falling and that I was on my own in the kitchen. There was certainly a temptation just to leave, to go out to my car and go home, however this did not seem appropriate or proper somehow and rather reluctantly my thoughts turned to trying to find NTD. The other more practical point was that I needed to sober up and I therefore filled and set the kettle which was near the sink. At this point I felt very drunk but could not have had more than 3 glasses of

champagne. That in itself began to make me feel very uncomfortable. Coffee would sober me up but also keep me awake and I therefore resolved to make some tea. On reflection, coffee would have been much better but then I could not really expect to be thinking clearly under all the circumstances.

112.   Because I had only seen NTD make coffee before it was necessary to begin looking in the cupboards and drawers for a mug, teapot and tea. It took me some time to realise that the ornate Oriental wooden box near the kettle was an old Chinese tea carrier. There must have been 12 different varieties of tea, some in their original packaging and some just in bags. In short, I made a pot of tea but it was only as I began to pour the hot water from the kettle into the teapot that I realised my hand was shaking, quite violently and uncontrollably. My instinct was to put the kettle down and to use my left hand to clutch the pot and use my right hand to try and steady the pot as I tried to pour it out; but to my surprise both hands were shaking just as much.

MAN SEES DEVIL AND GOES INTO SHOCK.

113.   Some of my thoughts were still rationale – realising that I would spill tea everywhere if I tried to take it to the table, I took one of the chairs and placed it near the sink and sat down. For the second time that evening I began to feel faint, lightheaded and very weak. I began some breathing exercises, something learnt during meditation classes many years previously. Breathe in slowly through the nose – counting one, two, three, very slowly. Hold the breath – counting one, two, three, very slowly. Then exhale though the mouth – counting one, two, three, very slowly. Breath in slowly through the nose – counting one, two, three, very slowly. Hold the breath – counting one, two, three, very slowly. Then exhale though the mouth – counting one, two, three, very slowly. This began to calm me and the shaking became more controllable. The tea was cold by the time I took a drink.

114.   For the first time that evening it occurred to me I should call my wife. Once I am heading home I would normally call her and tell her when she could expect me home. But on this occasion this did not seem a good idea – tell her everything, tell her nothing, tell her something in between? The hostess is drunk/drugged and missing – the butler/man servant has been taken to hospital in an ambulance. Oh yes and I just saw the Devil on the branch of an Oak tree crouching above a gently swinging noose! Without uttering a word these thoughts began to make me agitated and I began the breathing exercises again. Breath in slowly through the nose – counting one, two, three, very slowly. Hold the breath – counting one, two, three, very slowly. Then exhale though the mouth – counting one, two, three, very slowly. Breath in slowly through the nose – counting one, two, three, very slowly. Hold the breath – counting one, two, three, very slowly. Then exhale though the mouth – counting one, two, three, very slowly.

115.   My focus turned once again to finding NTD. In her state she could be anywhere – maybe she needed an ambulance as well. It was dark outside as I began to re boil the kettle to make hot tea, now in a slightly calmer state. Where could she have gone to? Could she still be outside? If so, it was too dark to start looking for her. I know I tried to calmly rationalise when and where I had last seen her. This simply made me more agitated again – the last time I could remember seeing her was outside by the table when the ambulance took Peter away. Could she have gone in the ambulance with Peter? That made sense but then I was sure I saw her walking slightly unsteadily back to the kitchen as the ambulance began to drive away. She beckoned me with her hand to follow, a slow gentle gesture and she knew I had seen it, as she turned straight away and walked into the kitchen. But then what?

116.   For some reason, the first place that seemed sensible to try was the Retreat. We had been there before as described in some detail above. But could I find it again? The main hall and stairs were lit, but I had no recollection of anyone turning on the lights. With a little difficulty I began to take the stairs and before I got to the first

landing I heard a muffled sound, from which at the time I was certain came from somewhere upstairs. I called out her name and for some reason I used her surname "Mrs Trewelyn-Digby" instead of Natalie. Somehow that familiarity did not seem appropriate anymore. I heard the sound once more as I got onto the first floor landing but it was impossible to say what it was, or from where it came. There was no lighting on in the upstairs hallway and it took me a little while to locate the light switch.

117. **[Note to reader – begin playing Low Deep T-Feelings 4 U –** *as loudly as possible*] It seemed to dawn upon me that my search for NTD needed to be systematic and methodical. I could spend hours roaming the floors. So although I felt reasonably certain that the sounds had not come from there I began by looking in each of the rooms of the first floor. It was in the third room that I entered that whatever it was that I had been drugged with began to kick in – and my word it kicked in. The effect came over me very quickly and became very pronounced within a minute or so. The wall-paper in the room came alive with an energy and light I had never experienced before. The crown symbols in dark red stepped off the wall and began to move rhythmically to the extremely loud music that had begun to play. And then there he was, a big black singer who sounded just like Barry White, only singing something more modern – a booming base voice that came straight from his soul – and there he was in the room – singing. "Feelings, feelings for you babe. Feelings, feelings for you, babe. Feelings, feelings for you, babe. When I met with you, babe, always thought I knew, babe everything I had to do to make you stay. Now you've gone away, oh it's not a happy day, baby. I guess I never did enough to make you stay. Want to let you know I never did enough to make you stay. I want to let you know I still got feelings for you baby, never gotten over you. Feelings, feelings for you babe, I still got feelings for you, baby."

118. And there I was dancing crazily in front of this man singing "Feelings, feelings for you, babe, I still got feelings for you." The beat was intense, hypnotic and I just kept moving. Dancing, moving,

dancing in a way I had never danced before, to music I had never listened to before. But I liked it.

119.   Although the birth is as clear and real to me as this paper and biro that I clutch, it seems likely that I may have to accept that there was no birth of a baby on 21 June 2014. However, I maintain that I believe NTD gave birth whilst the music was playing and the frenzied party ensued in the upper rooms of Rippleswade Hall. NTD moved very slowly to the music, and as I began to move more quickly she began to hold her midriff and twice bent over double and gave a silent scream. Although by this stage the music was so loud she could well have screamed the room down, it just would not have been heard over the music. As the song played on the line "Still got feelings for you baby" was repeated over and over again and as they were, NTD collapsed into the far corner of the room, by the small lamp table, the lamp was knocked over but was still working, and lying on the floor as it did, it had the effect of illuminating the birth in a most peculiar way. "Still got, still got feelings for you babe." NTD was slouched in the corner with her legs wide apart, knees raised and wrists resting uncomfortably on the knees. Her hands kept moving from on her knees to pushing hard downwards on the floor and then flying up to her head as if trying to release a vice gripping her temples.

120.   The baby almost flew out and within seconds was wrapped in a blanket and was being rocked by NTD in time to the music. It was a boy but I cannot tell you how I knew that, with a full head of red curly hair and despite the music and the dancing the baby would not take its eyes off NTD. She just sat in the corner gently rocking and it seemed to me she was crying very gently but very deeply. There was a lot of blood flowing onto the carpet and the way it was illuminated by the fallen lamp made it look like a river delta, beginning in her womb. At some point, as she continued to rock the baby, Satan knelt down in the blood and stroked the baby's hair, leant forward and kissed his forehead then took him up in his arms and carried him away. NTD just kept rocking and crying and her

arms were in a position as if she were still holding the baby. Without an explanation the blood disappeared and NTD took my hand – rose up and began to dance as if nothing had happened. It was some time shortly after this that I must have collapsed.

121.   It is stated that the police evidence is incontrovertible – there was no birth on 21 June and of course there was no baby. It was never my intention that NTD would have to be medically examined and her reported distress of having to undergo such an examination is equally distressing to me. But I will go to my grave knowing I saw what I saw. Whatever happened to me that night, be it a psychotic episode as some have suggested, or drug induced hallucination, that is what I saw.

122.   I must remain candid and state here that it remains possible in my mind that the birth I believe I witnessed was real. I cannot say otherwise. So much happened that night it would be foolish to dismiss anything out of hand. On the one hand you have a delusional old fool and on the other a highly reputable police team with specialist crime scene investigators. I am not a fool and I can well see my predicament. I have seen the medical evidence and it is clear that NTD did not give birth that night; nor indeed any other night it is never easy proving the negative. I can prove I am married by producing a birth certificate. Proving I am not married is a whole different matter. All of this I well understand.

123.   As referred to above, I must have collapsed at some stage, because from dancing with the singer the next thing I remember is waking up very groggily face down on the carpet next to a chaise longue in a completely different part of the Hall with my mouth resting on a high heeled shoe. The music and the words were still pounding in my head and I will never know for certain whether the music was in fact still playing. As I began to regain consciousness all I could focus on with the music still pounding was whose shoe it was that I had been dribbling on. It was very difficult to get up and for some time I just lay there with my eyes closed and feeling very thirsty. It was

whilst I lay there that the coil repeatedly consumed my thoughts like a feverish dervish. The coil subsumed everything else. The coil became all. At that time I could not say where in the coil I was. That troubled me, but I could see the coil very clearly. The coil was the solution to the universe, no more, no less.

124. As I very slowly and gingerly rolled onto my back it became apparent that I had lost all my clothing bar my boxer shorts and socks. Barely conscious, nearly naked in a part of a client's house I should probably not have been in, it slowly began to make sense to get out of there. But I could hardly return home in my boxer shorts and socks and tell Joanne what an interesting evening it had been. A new search began – this time for my clothes. But first I had to have water.

125. The room in which I found myself was, I believe, NTD's bedroom. There was a door within the room that led into a very luxurious en suite bathroom, with a fireplace, free-standing bath, a black marble power shower, a sink and bidet. The chrome towel warmers were super sized and the whole room sparkled as though it were just recently installed. Water never tasted so good but as I washed my face and looked into the mirror above the sink I could see that there was dry blood in my mouth. That frightened me. I rolled my tongue around my mouth and could find no sensitive area, nothing to indicate from where the blood might have come. I could only conclude that it was not my blood and that gave me some comfort.

126. The bathroom cabinet mirror opened and had a small cabinet behind it and amongst the various items was some mouth wash. As I replaced it I began to look more closely at some of the other items – mainly tablets in small brown plastic bottles with prescription labels all made out in the name of NTD. There were bottles of Depakote, Lithium, Aricept, and Klonopin. All the prescriptions were made out in her name, for the first time it occurred to me that all may not be what it seemed with NTD, she clearly had problems.

127.   Something moved in the bedroom, I heard a noise and this startled me, so I left the en suite quickly, assuming it was NTD. Never before I have been so relieved and then so shocked. NTD was in the bed and lying under her was the Devil. They were either wrestling or making love but under her, pinned or being seduced was the Devil. NTD looked up at me but she did not seem surprised or bothered, indeed it was not clear that it had registered for her that I was in the room, she looked half conscious, her eyes were barely open and her hair was even more tousled now. She was sitting on the torso of Satan and her hands grasped his arms and had them pressed to the bed. The scene was strangely arousing. NTD was wearing an unbuttoned mans shirt and it was then that I noticed that the Devil had blood in his mouth and seemed to be grinning or maybe he was grimacing.

128.   I must have passed out again because when I regained consciousness NTD was kneeling beside me trying to revive me. She was still wearing the shirt I had seen her in earlier but now it was partially buttoned. She had cupped my neck in one hand and had a glass of water in the other. She spoke to me in a very calm and soft way, "Mr Whibley, are you alright? Please, try and drink some water." As I came round I realised to my horror that I was still only wearing my boxer shorts and socks.

129.   It is highly doubtful that I was fit to drive but nevertheless it is the case that I left Rippleswade Hall by car. I must agree that there was then a large gap in my memory of what happened the following morning. I can recall getting into my car and I recall that as I pulled away NTD stood in a barely buttoned shirt waving an arm and sat next to me in the car was Satan, gently holding the red-haired baby. That I can clearly remember. Everything else is a blank until I pulled up into the car park at The Vulcan & Griffin. It was my local, approximately 25 minutes drive from where I live. I got out of my car in the car park just before midday but the drive from

Rippleswade Hall should have taken no longer than 2 hours (even accounting for heavy traffic) and I had left just after dawn. There are therefore approximately five hours unaccounted for – perhaps I was driving around, although that is highly unlikely as I still had a quarter tank of petrol. What was clear was that Satan was no longer with me.

130.   I have frequented The Vulcan & Griffin for over 30 years, often stopping for a drink before getting home after a site visit. The owner is a Mike Swain, a convivial Dublin publican. Nadia has been a barmaid there for three years or so and there is no denying she is extremely attractive with a tendency to dress provocatively. She has a stunning figure so some may argue it would be difficult to not dress provocatively. There were various rumours that she was having an affair with Mike, that she was married back in the Czech Republic, that she had three babies all of which she had sold. In short, Nadia is a beautiful eastern European girl with strawberry blonde hair, green eyes and a beautiful figure. On the morning I am describing she was wearing black leggings, boots and a baggy white tee shirt with some black and white picture and some printed words I cannot recall on it.

131.   I still fail to see that what allegedly did or did not happen at The Vulcan & Griffin that morning has anything to do with NTD and the allegations that have been made against me. It may be that I did fall or stumble as I walked from my car to the Snug entrance but I have no recollection of knocking my head. If someone did see that happen then all I can say is that it might have happened. At the end of the day it was Nadia who put her arm around me first, I am not an old fool and if she did that it was in all likelihood to steady me or support me. If I misinterpreted that gesture, there were some highly extenuating circumstances.

132.   There cannot be many pubs where you can get a pint of Theakston's XB on tap, a serving of Suffolk Pond Pudding with cream and ice cream on the last Tuesday of the month and sit by an open fire and

look through the Snug window to waves crashing on the rocks only 20 metres away. On a winter's day when the sea is violent it really bears no comparison to any other pub I have been to. When the odd Antipodean sits in the Snug and recalls some beach in warmer climes he has to be reminded that you cannot eat Suffolk Pond Pudding in summer heat – it would kill you. If I had to be stuck in one place for the rest of my life it would be The Vulcan & Griffin – without any hesitation or doubt. That is where my Wake will be.

133. Long friendships are in part about shared experiences that cannot be taken away and cannot be re-created. The regulars at V&G had many lock-ins and Sussex Pond Puddings to ruminate over. There was the night over 20 years ago when the American cast of Cling and about 18 singers and dancers bundled into the Snug about 9:30 p.m. one cold and wind swept winter evening asking if they could get food and drinks. Mike had not been the owner for very long at that time and the prospect of 18 covers for food and drink on a quiet weekday meant his eyes nearly popped out or was it the ample cleavage of Dolores L Belle? To a man they all drank Long Island Iced Teas and they were thirsty. Mike had only just finished making the first round when they were ordering the next one. The strange thing was that at no stage during the evening did any one of them check the price of anything they were consuming. They had at least 4 or 5 drinks each and did these people eat. With no sign of them leaving at about 11:30 p.m. Dolores approached Mike and asked if she could sing for her supper. The beaming Mike immediately went pale and simply stuttered. One of the men began playing the piano and Dolores began to hum. Straight away the few of us that were still there fell silent and Dolores began to sing the most moving rendition I have ever heard of *Strange Fruit*. Even the piano player stopped after a few bars. It sent a cold shiver down my spine and the hairs on my neck literally stood to attention. To pick up the mood a little the next song was *Summertime* and two of the other ladies sang with Dolores and by the end of that track most of the 18 were by the piano either singing, playing or dancing. They went through a full repertoire and they did not finish until 4:00 a.m. – they had drunk Mike out of white

spirits and then they just jumped into their bus and left as suddenly as they had arrived. They did not pay a penny for anything but for weeks afterwards Mike had a huge beam on his face. The most over the top theatre review could not have done this evening justice. It was a concert given by 18 talented musicians to eight people at the V&G and quite simply you were there that evening or you were not. There was Mike and two bar staff, then myself and Johnny Sturridge, Owen and Jasper and Olde Feck.

134. The unpleasant incident of Miele's breakdown did not reflect well on any of the regulars. On reflection it was silly and possibly cruel but it was never intended to be so. It probably was me that started it all off. Miele had been learning English for some time and took it very seriously. She saw it as an important gateway to much better things. For some reason I do not now recall, I thought it would be amusing to become an Etonian East End spiv when ordering drinks from Miele, whose English was actually very good. It went something along the lines of, "Watcha cock, a pint of Jaeger splosh tweakle and how's a dandy." Maldon had burst out laughing when he overheard this and the sport was born. All of a sudden The V&G was full of London gangsters and Pearly Queens – "A quart of tincture and a bag of how's your father." The more irritated she became the more outlandish the orders became. Most of the regulars started to frequent the V&G more often and especially when Miele had a shift. "Tweakle, a flagon of anymore." It just kept snow balling – there were Arthurian Knights, Newcastle likely lads, Scousers, Brummies but when I saw her in tears in the back hallway, I knew instantly that the "sport" had been cruel and hurtful. If we were honest we all already knew that, but the cruelty was subsumed by the laughter we derived from the situation. "Quaffing fluid ye buxom wench and a yard of palest male for. Imbibing potions you beauty and a tippin of facks." No-one could have foreseen that Miele would become so distressed by all of this but to walk out without so much as a goodbye perhaps made us all feel a little less comfortable. It is understandable that she never came back to the V&G but to a

man every regular sincerely wished that she had – we would have treated her like royalty, of that I am quite sure.

135.   It is important that I set out what it is others say that happened in the morning of 22 June 2014. This is because at that time I can recall only parts of what happened. It was said that I tore in like a hurricane, drank very quickly three pints of Guinness, not my preferred drink in summer, then helped myself in the kitchen to a leg of ham with pickles and relish and then proceeded to dance and sing by the piano, unaccompanied and very much on my own. Apparently I was singing, over and over again, "Still got feelings for you, babe, still got, still got feelings for you, babe." By all accounts the dancing was not at all bad, if a little eccentric; a sort of slow shuffle with hands held up to the chest, a bit like a boxer, with sudden and jerky movements of the shoulders backwards and forwards. But always the slow shuffle. I have been made aware subsequently that on a number of occasions Miele tried to persuade me to sit down but I have no recollection of that whatsoever.

136.   I also have no recollection whatsoever about drinking three pints of Guinness, I must have been thirsty. Also, no recollection at all about the leg of ham and pickle. Mike made sure it all went on my tab; the leg of ham was expensive.

137.   Shown to me now and marked "**BOW 6** " is a letter dated 18 September 2014 from Palton Police Station asking if I would be prepared to voluntarily provide a DNA sample in relation to their investigation into the "incidents" at Rippleswade Hall on 21 June 2014. The receipt of this letter came as a complete surprise to me as this was the first occasion there had been any indication from anyone that the matter was being looked into. At the time I received the letter I had no idea as to why I was being asked to provide a DNA sample, obviously I do now. As per the contents of the letter I telephoned the station the same morning I received the letter and spoke with PC Sally Norman and arranged to attend at the station the following day. Palton is approx. a 30 minute drive due west from my home and is

not particularly local to me and it is certainly some distance from Rippleswade Hall.

138. For some reason that I am not sure I can explain, I chose not to tell Joanne about the letter, nor my providing a DNA sample voluntarily. She would probably have objected and rightly so. But for me, this felt like a final tenuous connection to Rippleswade Hall.

139. Upon arrival at the station I met PC Norman. It has to be said that she looked like the twin sister of NTD – only with her hair tied up, in police uniform and wearing a police hat. On first seeing her, I nearly blurted out "Nathalie". PC Norman sensed my unease/surprise but conducted herself very professionally. I was taken into a small side room and PC Norman herself took a swab sample from my mouth. This was placed into a hard plastic tube and details were written on both the tube and the clear plastic bag into which it was placed. Throughout that visit and even now I remain convinced that PC Norman was in fact NTD.

140. I do not believe that it is so peculiar that I should try to make contact with NTD some six months after the dinner to try and clarify what exactly happened that night. After all, it nearly cost me my marriage, I have been for counselling, seen a psychiatrist and all I wished to try and establish was with what had I been drugged. Some of the medication in her bathroom cabinet is extremely powerful. I remain adamant that what I experienced that evening was the result of my unwilling imbibing of some substance or drug by which I was rendered powerless and which resulted in a type of psychotic episode.

141. Under all of the circumstances I did not think it would be appropriate to contact NTD directly and as my work was completed I did not have any reason to contact her on a professional basis. I felt that the only way I could reasonably speak with her would be to "accidentally" chance upon her when she was outside of Rippleswade Hall. The one thing I recalled with clarity was the

freshly ground coffee – she had mentioned the coffee merchant at Padchester and I determined that if I waited near the coffee supplier long enough at some point she would be there to pick up supplies. I was sure she had mentioned she get a regular supply fortnightly.

142.   Jack Pempler is an old friend. We first got to know each other when I appointed him as a private detective, almost 20 years ago to undertake covert surveillance work. I contacted Jack and pretended this was a new piece of work for him. The instructions were clear; to find out on what days and at what time NTD went to the coffee merchant. My sense was that she was very much a creature of habit and that Jack could quickly establish when I could bump into her. Jack suggested he casually ask the proprietors but I explained I was not keen to arouse any suspicion. This needed to be done very discreetly.

143.   It was more than a little surprising that it took Jack nearly two months before he came back to me. He is extremely thorough and his report was short and to the point. He sent an email "First and fourth Wednesday's of the month between 09:00 and 10:30 a.m. – Regards Jack". So there I had it – I now just needed to plot how this would work. There was no doubt she would be surprised to see me and I did not want to startle her. I needed her to feel at ease when we met so I could engage her in conversation – a quick coffee perhaps or help her back to the car with her shopping. This needed to be planned with precision and it needed to be flexible, I would need to be reactive with what was happening, to be able to roll with things as they occurred. What if she did not want to speak with me? What if she became agitated? What if she screamed? What if she pretended not to know me? Almost anything was possible and I needed to think through as many possible scenarios and work out what I should do and say.

144.   The first attempt to "bump" into NTD at the coffee supplier was, on reflection, poorly executed, particularly given the time and planning that had gone into it. Bad planning and bad luck made the trip a

farce. On 6 October 2014 I drove to Padchester. The journey from my home to Padchester should normally take just over an hour and I had allowed an hour and a half. However due to an accident on the Sedgbury bypass I was delayed in traffic for 45 minutes. What I had not realised was that the first Tuesday of the month was a market day and the main car park at the top of the town was full, and I had to drive, slowly in the congestion, down to the overflow car park at the bottom of town. The walk from there up the hill to Ryled Street must be over half a mile and for a man in my condition that is a serious work out. By the time I was halfway up Ryled Street and taking a much-needed breather with a bottle of cold water I had purchased at the newsagent, it was 10:35 am and the window to meet NTD was almost certainly lost.

145. It dawned on me as I stood there that this might actually be a blessing. Not one contingency had been thought through by me, not properly. What if I was early/late? What if NTD was early/late/not there at all? Did I plan to be in the coffee shop, outside the coffee shop, round the corner from the coffee shop? Would I approach her directly, pretend to bump into her by accident or drop something in front of her? Should I suggest a coffee, lunch or a future meeting? I needed to consider her reaction. Would she recognise me immediately, pretend to vaguely remember me or not remember me at all? Would she be friendly, aloof, embarrassed or aggressive? None of this had been thought through in the way it should have been. Yes, I had given it some thought, but not nearly enough and I began to feel acutely embarrassed as I drank my water, but at the same time realising this afforded me an opportunity to properly plan this, with a precision that all my professional training and experience could muster.

146. It was just as I began to continue heading up Ryled Street when I saw NTD walking, and still the only way to describe it was languidly, up the hill on the other side of the street. Ryled Street was pedestrianised on market days. My heart jumped and began to race. NTD was wearing black leather trousers, which were very flattering

to her figure and I recalled the comment of the man at the train station in Vietnam. She was wearing a baggy coral pink mohair pullover and she had on a pearl necklace around her neck. NTD must have recently been back from abroad as she looked much browner than when I had seen her before but her hair was exactly as I remembered it. Not unsurprisingly she was attracting a lot of attention, not least from two teenage boys who were slouching on a bench she had just passed. I could not hear what was said but they appeared to call after her, but she just carried on walking oblivious to the fuss she was creating. I began to realise I was not the only person trying to make contact with NTD.

147.   Had she seen me? There was no way to know, and I instinctively began to follow her, but on the opposite side of the street and discretely behind her. She had a Louis Vuitton handbag on her arm and she was carrying a brown paper shopping bag, like an old-fashioned grocery bag, in the other arm, and loosely held against her chest.

148.   My heart, if anything, was racing faster than when I first saw her a few minutes earlier, or was it the uphill climb? My thinking was immediately much less coherent. Should I call out, run after her, or just follow at a distance? The first two options were not immediately practical under the circumstances. A little further up Ryled Street NTD turned and entered into a small family run chemist. I waited across the street trying to gather my composure and thoughts. Although a late autumnal morning, it was warm in the sun and foolishly I decided to purchase another bottle of water. By the time I got back to be watching the chemist NTD was gone. After a few minutes I walked past the chemist three times and then went in, NTD was definitely not there. I did think about asking the young lady behind the counter about NTD but in that instance I could not think of any way of speaking about her without appearing odd. As is so often the case much came to me afterwards. I could have pretended she had dropped something further down the street or that I was her

husband – I did rather like that. I also made a mental note to go back to this pharmacy as the young assistant was strikingly attractive.

149. As I left the chemist I am reasonably sure that I saw NTD driving off in a black Aston Martin Vanquis, with the soft top down. A more striking image of beauty and wealth I cannot envisage. She must have been parked just off Ryled Street, probably on Praved Lane, but, as I discovered later, that has restricted parking on market days, but I never found a better explanation. There I had it – moments earlier she was there and now she was gone and it occurred to me immediately I would have to wait at least a fortnight before the next possible accidental meeting could take place.

151. Did NTD have voodoo? Perhaps she did, because she was much in my dreams and too much in my head generally. In my dreams she is lying on my chest and cuddling up to me in the way comfortable married couples do. We were always talking about things I could not divine but always she laughed and found me very witty. Some dreams are better than others.

152. This sighting of NTD redoubled my determination to meet and speak with her. What had become clear was that this project needed to be planned meticulously. This had been a chance sighting but it appeared that Jed's information was reasonably accurate. I determined to not let the dust settle and I vowed to speak with her in two weeks. That evening at Rippleswade Hall had eaten away at me and had significantly impacted my life and I deserved some sort of explanation. My psychologist had talked about a form of acceptance leading to closure but my relationship with Joanne had been irreparably harmed. A trust that had built up over 30 years of conjugal fidelity had been lost, destroyed, brutalised and damaged forever – you cannot unring a bell as they say. But how can I deny accusations when for large parts of the evening I have no recollection whatsoever of what went on? I have recounted in as much detail as possible the events as I recall them.

153.   The basic plan was simple. An early departure to Padchester, maybe even an overnight stay, and to be outside or near the coffee merchant for 8:30 a.m. until NTD arrived. I decided to go to Padchester one week before the intended "meeting" and try and find somewhere I could discretely wait in order not to draw attention to myself. It hardly made sense to just stand outside the coffee merchant for maybe an hour and a half. A plan began to form. I stayed overnight in Padchester on the Monday of the week before our intended meeting. It did not take long to locate a small teashop six or seven doors down on the opposite side of the street from the coffee merchant. There was one window table at the teashop from where one could clearly and discretely see the frontage of the coffee merchant. It became clear that as I had no idea from which direction NTD would approach the shop – my best opportunity to "meet" her was to bump into her as she left the coffee merchant. It did occur to me that I should spend a couple of weeks properly staking this out but by then it had become for me a matter of some urgency. The other issue was that the following Tuesday was not a market day and the town centre would be much quieter.

154.   It was obvious that this plan would only work if I had the window seat at the teashop. That was imperative. It was the only table from which the frontage of the coffee merchant could be clearly seen. But it did not appear that the tea shop was the sort of establishment at which you could reserve a table. So it became clear I would need to get to the tea shop in good time and well before I first expected to see NTD. It looked as though large pots of tea were going to be in order, or a very slow full English breakfast. On thinking this through I realised there was no point me sitting there drinking cup after cup of tea – sooner or later I would need to use the facilities and once that train was started. Some serious thought was given by me to having a catheter fitted – every eventuality possible needed to be considered and as odd as this may sound the idea made perfect sense. However, I could arrive at no medical grounds for personally getting a catheter fitted.

155.   It still surprises me that with all this planning things could still go wrong. I drove up to Padchester late on the following Monday afternoon and had booked in again at the The Queen's Head, an old coaching inn in the middle of Padchester for bed and breakfast. It was simple really, by having the breakfast at The Queen's Head, I would be full and the breakfast at the tea shop would be easy to prolong. It was necessary to get to the teashop by 7:45 a.m. a full one hour and 15 minutes before NTD was expected to arrive at the coffee merchant, at the earliest.

BIG CHANGE OF PLAN

156.   It is hard for me to indulge in a full English, indeed that has been the case for many years. Medical advice informs that my cholesterol levels are on the high side of normal and that porridge or bran flakes should be the order of the day and they have been for many years. So having two full English breakfasts placed in front of you within an hour on the same morning seemed excessive. The second breakfast was not after all to eat but to play with whilst I awaited NTD. Two things dawned on me as the second breakfast was served to me in the teashop (1) this could take up to three hours if NTD did not appear until nearly 10:00 a.m., which was well within the bounds of possibility; and (2) having planned the sighting so carefully no thought had been given as to what I would actually say to NTD. "Oh hi, it's you. Well well, Long time no see."

157.   Sometimes in life things can take a while to properly sink in, to register. When I saw the lady with the blonde bob, tightly fitting designer dress and heels go into the coffee merchant at around 8:45 a.m. it had not occurred to me for a moment that NTD might have changed her appearance. Why would it? So there I was, exactly as planned, having deliberately taken an age to order breakfast and now sitting in front of a full English with eggs easy over, a side order of black pudding, toast with a pot of tea and condiment jar of English mustard that it was only as NTD left the coffee merchant, down the four steps that led up to the front door that it hit me BAM,

KAPPOW, like in a Batman comic strip that there was the lady I so needed to speak with.

158.   I tried to leave the teashop as quickly as I could. However, having laboured to recognise NTD, my escape was more hurried than planned and at the front door a very elderly couple were slowly entering the tea shop and until they had passed the entrance was blocked!

159.   Upon leaving the tea shop NTD was moving slowly down Ryled Street on the opposite side and now a good 40 yards ahead of me heading towards the main car park. For various reasons she looked different than I recalled. She was wearing heels, which I had not seen her in before, and this made her seem both taller and slimmer than I remembered. Her bust seemed much fuller, she was wearing a tight dress and her legs seemed longer and more athletically defined. She had always worn loose clothing during our previous meetings. Something did not seem right and it was at this point that the first doubts crept into my head; although this was clearly a well dressed lady there was nothing to indicate this was NTD other than her overall demeanour. Whilst, on a certain level this lady could be NTD there were some clear and accountable differences that could not be easily explained.

160.   It became necessary for me to do some breathing exercises to try and clear my head. Breath in slowly through the nose – counting one, two, three very slowly. Hold the breath – counting one, two, three, very slowly. Then exhale though the mouth – counting one, two, three, very slowly. Breath in slowly through the nose – counting one, two, three very slowly. Hold the breath – counting one, two, three, very slowly. Then exhale though the mouth – counting one, two, three, very slowly. It was not easy to try and stay calm and go through the scenarios that had so occupied me over the last few weeks.

161.   All I could think to do now was to follow NTD at a discrete distance and try and buy myself some time. This was not a scenario I had even begun to register let alone plan for. It quickly became clear that NTD was indeed heading towards the car park and it therefore seemed that time was of the essence, so I began to slowly run in the same direction as NTD but staying on the opposite side of the street. It is difficult to say precisely what did happen next, but events suggest that I tripped or fell at the entrance of the car park, just as NTD had begun paying her parking fare. I must have momentarily lost consciousness as by the time I came round a very helpful young couple and an elderly lady were leaning over me asking if I was alright and someone suggesting an ambulance be called as I had clearly knocked my head. Trying to dust myself off and refusing the ambulance, I rather unsteadily made it to my feet and then sat on the nearby bench. There in the background watching at a discrete distance was NTD, and as our views met she seemed to turn a little hurriedly to her car, and it was the black Aston Martin Vanquis again. I could do nothing more than sit on the bench and watch her almost in slow motion get into her car and drive off. There was a spot of blood on my shirt and it took a little while to register that I had cut my temple when I fell and there was now some blood in my eye as well. I tried to call out to NTD, but with the running and the fall my throat was dry and a rather unusual gurgle came out. It was at that point that the young couple agreed they should call an ambulance.

162.   There it was, as it turned out, my last opportunity to discuss with NTD what had happened on 21 June 2014. She disappeared around the corner in her car and I assume back to Rippleswade Hall. After this episode in Padchester Jed made some further discrete enquiries on my behalf and it appeared that only two weeks after this meeting NTD had gone abroad and seemed to have no fixed intention of returning. She had gone to a chalet in Switzerland, in the same village the painter Balthus used to live, Rossiniere. It appeared she had also been unsettled by whatever occurred on that fateful night

as I subsequently learned that Rippleswade Hall had been put on the market for sale, including all its contents.

163.   It is nearly 9 months since the events detailed above occurred but I remember the 21 June 2014 as though it all happened yesterday. There is a clarity to my recollections that I have not known before, not on my wedding day and not at my father's funeral. I can say with a high degree of certainty that the events I have recounted above are both accurate and faithful to what occurred. Although some may say this is fanciful, the ramblings of a mad man, I saw what I saw. What meaning or significance these events have is a matter for others. What I have been instructed to do is to recount the facts as accurately and in as much detail as I can, and I have done this to the best of my knowledge and belief. There has been no embellishment or prosaic presentation, I have told my version of events with candour and honesty. I saw what I saw.

164.   I certify that the contents of this statement are true to the best of my knowledge and belief.

The Voices

Momma Whibley: *I had no idea how painful a miscarriage could be. Your father so wanted a daughter – it was a girl – we would have called her Sasha.*

The Brigadier: Your mother. Me. Nothing seedy.

Momma Whibley: I spoke with Joyce earlier today. She said how much she had enjoyed seeing you. She always comments that you have such a nice smile, a warm face. But I told her, "He can be as hard as steel."

The Brigadier: Standing room only from Naggasha. Standing room only.

The Brigadier: Bitch dead, long live bastard.

Momma Whibley: So you fell for a girl, indeed you ended up marrying her, because you liked her handwriting. In fact, more specifically, because you really liked the "cute" way she inserted a squashed "o" over her "i"s and "j"s. I didn't realise you were so shallow.

The Brigadier: Red-hot ice drops fell on head as if standing under Hell.

Momma Whibley: Your father's finest hour was WWII. He didn't fight in it of course, but we were having our Friday night drink down at The Rose & Crown, you remember you used to sneak in there when you were 16 to ogle at the bar girls. One evening a German couple were there having a drink, never seen before or since. Old Ned set about them proper as he would say. He started asking them about the war and asked whether they had met Hitler. The couple were very composed and spoke good English. Anyway, after a while the German woman said "Please, please we just want to have a quiet drink, we are not ready for this". Quick as a flash your father said, "Neither was Poland." It brought the house down, even the German couple laughed. It was talked about for years. That's the story you should have told at his funeral. Whenever that story was recounted your father's eyes always lit up.

Momma Whibley: You used to tuck old letters into books. I found a letter from Ishani not so long ago in a poetry book. Must be over 35 years ago as it seemed to be written just after you got your results from Aberyswyth. She said not to

86

worry and she would always love you and be there for you. She meant it at the time Millie, but not now. You have to let that go. What are you going to do? Turn up on her doorstep with the letter waiving it in her face and reminding her that she said she loved you and would always be there for you. She won't even remember the letter Millie.

The Brigadier: *Burma. Bloody hot. Jungle. Trekking. Bloody humid.*
Your mother. Me. Not clever. W never knew.
Rare beauty. No control. No regrets.

The Brigadier: *One regret. She stayed with W.*

Sasha: *We never met did we, but we were blood? Here I am!*

The Brigadier: *Knew it was bad. Figures moving on the Polaroid – they bloody moved I tell you. Bad trip, very bad.*

Moma Whibley: *You were such a bonny baby, always laughing and giggling – so happy. What happened? Was it us?*

The Brigadier: *The olde see youth in everyone, and youth see the age.*

Momma Whibley: *It was hardly science rocket, as our local cab driver was fond of saying.*

The Brigadier: *Spectrum people are everywhere. Some diagnosed, some not. Either way, highly fucking dangerous people. They knock and rattle in startled chambers. Oddbod, Needie Wierdo and Clingee.*

NAME:	Mr. Barrington Olivier Whibley
DATE OF BIRTH:	29 February 1946
ADDRESS:	Willow Cottage
	Norton Farm Road
	Favering Creechurch
	Dorset
	DT34 3LU
COUNTY COURT:	Not as yet known
CASE NO	Not as yet known
CLAIMANT SOLICITOR	Not as yet known
REFERENCE:	Not as yet known
DEFENDANT INSURERS:	Not as yet known
REFERENCE:	Not as yet known
MY REFERENCE	4974-BWhibley-rpt001
REPORT DATED:	30 March 2015

(1) INTRODUCTION

(1.1) THE WRITER

My name is Thesper Andreas Carrington. I am a Chartered Clinical Psychologist. My specialist field is psychological trauma and psychosis an area within which I have worked over the past twenty-five years. As required under the Civil Procedure Rules full details of my qualifications are set out at Appendix 1 to this report.

(1.2) INSTRUCTIONS

The case concerns an unusual set of facts that occurred on 21 June 2014 and which are set out in fuller detail below. Originally I had been instructed by Mr. Whibley to investigate whether Mr. Whibley had suffered a formal psychological/psychiatric condition or whether what he had experienced was as a result of his involuntary taking some sort of hallucinatory drug and the effects and prognosis if appropriate. Subsequent to that initial instruction Mr. Whibley has been named in civil proceedings issued by Natalie Trelewyn-Digby and I have been retained by Mr. Whibley's lawyers to act as an independent expert into his psychological profile. I have been provided with Mr. Whibley's general practice notes and records.

(2) INVESTIGATION
(2.1) INTERVIEW
DATE OF INTERVIEW: 2 March 2015
ALSO INTERVIEWED: Mrs. Joanne Whibley (Wife)

(2.1.1) ON EXAMINATION
Mr. Whibley presented entirely appropriately and gave a clear and consistent account of the incidents leading up to and including the evening of 21 June 2014 and its impact upon him. Mr. Whibley was clearly distressed by the levels of anxiety he still experiences in relation to the events of 21 June 2014.

(2.1.2) THE INCIDENT AND SUBSEQUENT DEVELOPMENTS
On the 21 June 2014 Mr. Whibley attended a dinner party at Rippleswade Hall hosted by Natalie Trelewyn-Digby at which he was the only guest. Various events occurred that evening some of which appear to be common ground and some of which are disputed as between Mr. Whibley and Ms. Trelewyn-Digby. During recounting these events Mr. Whibley became very emotional so much so that at one point he became tearful and left the consulting room to compose himself. Although this did not last long it is clear that Mr. Whibley is still emotionally sensitive to the events of that evening. He expressed his surprise at the extent of his reaction. This is not unusual in cases such as this.

I have reviewed a copy of the draft witness statement of Mr. Whibley and this sets out in very full detail the events of the evening of 21 June 2014.

The significant features of the evening in Mr. Whibley's account are as follows:

1. He was the only guest at the dinner party
2. The man servant known as Peter collapsed
3. A local doctor was called
4. An ambulance left with Peter and the doctor

5. s. Trelewyn-Digby disappeared for prolonged periods leaving Mr. Whibley alone at Rippleswade Hall
6. Mr. Whibley saw both a noose and Satan in the Oak tree behind the outdoor dinner setting
7. Mr. Whibley then went into a trance like state and heard loud music – the same song played over and over
8. Mr. Whibley saw a singer performing in Rippleswade Hall
9. Mr. Whibley witnessed Ms. Trelewyn-Digby give birth to a baby boy
10. Mr. Whibley saw Satan take the newborn child
11. In the morning Mr. Whibley left by car with Satan and the baby
12. Mr. Whibley attended at The George & Vulture pub a local hostelry he frequented usually in the evening. It is alleged that he molested a female member of staff at The George & Vulture. Mr. Whibley has no recollection of this whatsoever.

It was only at the end of recounting these events that Mr. Whibley became very emotional. His wife was unable to comfort him to any degree.

It is now some nine months since the incident in question and Mr. Whibley has been unable to properly get over the events. Feelings of distress and anxiety have persisted since that evening. Up until 21 June Mr. Whibley described his psychological profile as normal and there had been no previous history of anxiety or depression.

Mr. Whibley finally arrived home to his wife at approx. 3:30 p.m. on 22 June 2014. Almost 24 hours after he had left for the dinner party. Mrs. Whibley described him as being extremely agitated and his behavior that day was uncharacteristically erratic. Mr. Whibley says that over the 48 hours after the dinner party there are large portions of time when he simply has no recollection at all of his actions. This includes the first 12 hours or so of his arrival home.

Mrs. Whibley explained that upon arrival home Mr. Whibley was only partially dressed and he insisted on taking a very long bath. For the last 30 years Mr. Whibley has always showered. He sang a few lines from a song over and over again. "Still got feelings still got feeling for you, baby." Mrs. Whibley explained that Mr. Whibley very rarely sings and this was not a song with which she was familiar.

Mr. and Mrs. Whibley normally go to bed at approx. 22:30 and have done so for many years. On the evening of 22 June Mr. Whibley stayed up until 2:30 a,m. the following morning. Once he had finished his bath Mr. Whibley sat in the rocking chair wrapped in a wet towel and just rocked. Mrs. Whibley attempted on a number of occasions to persuade him to come to bed but Mr. Whibley more or less ignored her. When he did finally get to bed he then slept for over 16 hours. Mr. Whibley can recall nothing of these events and his first recollection from leaving The George & Vulture pub was when he woke up at approx. 18:30 on 23 June.

When he awoke Mr. Whibley described his feelings as being bewildered and disorientated. He began to experience immediate flashbacks and Mrs. Whibley described Mr. Whibley as "not at all his normal self-tremulous and almost feverish". Mr. Whibley does not recall this. Mrs. Whibley became very concerned about Mr. Whibley's condition and arranged for the family GP Dr Kasim, to attend. He administered Mr. Whibley a reasonably strong sedative 30 mg of Amotriplin and Mr. Whibley then fell asleep not awaking again until 8:45 a.m. on the morning of 24 June 2014.

When Mr. Whibley awoke on 24 June he felt much improved but still "mildly bewildered and anxious" though nothing like as severe as in the previous 48 hours. Mrs. Whibley cancelled a number of work appointments and Mr. Whibley was subsequently off work for two weeks. Over this period he felt progressively calmer but he did visit his GP on two occasions to obtain prescriptions for further sedatives/tranquilizers. The medical records appear to be incomplete as I can find no record of what was prescribed.

In any event Mr. Whibley describes a slow but steady progress to normality with flash backs and anxiety attacks becoming less frequent and severe.

One significant effect is that Mr. Whibley details a high degree of anxiety when attending visits to locations he has not been to before. Mr. Whibley describes difficulty in sleeping the night before his sleep is broken and he wakes in the early hours and is unable to get back to sleep. After a bad night's sleep he finds driving longer distances can cause him distress as he is conscious that he is fatigued. This entails much more frequent stops and Mr. Whibley notes that his caffeine intake has significantly increased to deal with these situations. There are no issues arising when Mr. Whibley attends properties he has visited before and with which he is familiar.

Mr. and Mrs. Whibley described themselves as a reasonably social couple but were both very conscious that this had dropped off significantly as Mr. Whibley finds he is generally more fatigued and less inclined to socialize since the incident. Mr. Whibley described himself as an enthusiastic but untalented golfer and has not played since last June. He does not feel inclined to play and feels it is unlikely that he will play again. Golf had been his main hobby and he has now given up his club membership.

There have been intermittent flash back episodes when Mr. Whibley feels as though he has been "transported back into the night of 21 June". These are intense episodes and generally occur when he is trying to get back to sleep after he has already been asleep. The key features of these flashbacks are the loud music Satan being present in some context and Rippleswade Hall being very prevalent. It is interesting that Mr. Whibley makes almost no mention of Ms. Trelewyn-Digby in these episodes. During these flashbacks Mr. Whibley becomes almost feverish and Mrs. Whibley has noticed that his left hand involuntarily twitches. These episodes can last for up to ten minutes and afterwards Mr. Whibley will appear dazed and distressed. On eight occasions in total since 21 June Mr. Whibley has attended at his GP generally seeking medication to assist him in sleeping and/or to reduce his anxiety. Mr. Whibley has been keen to avoid becoming too reliant on medication to assist with his condition. His GP has suggested counselling which Mr. Whibley followed up with limited success. Mr. Whibley does not have private medical insurance.

Mr. Whibley has become in his own words "obsessed" with what happened to him on 21 June. He remains adamant that he was given some sort of opiate/hallucinatory drug. Regrettably, he did not obtain a blood test until many weeks after the incident and those tests were negative. One of the main reasons for arranging the first of these consultations was to explore if there is any further evidence that could be provided as to what happened. On this issue he has shown signs of irritability as he feels strongly that he needs to understand what happened to him. His own enquiries although extensive have not been helpful in this regard and if anything have caused additional stress and anxiety.

There was no indication of symptoms of emotional numbing. Mr. Whibley calls himself a "closet Buddhist" and has a very grounded view on life generally. There is no sense of a foreshortened future.

His wife attended part of the interview and it was noticeable that she is very concerned about him. Mr. Whibley seemed a lot more relaxed when on his own and was much freer and forthright. He seemed much more measured in his responses when Mrs. Whibley was with him. Mrs. Whibley presented as being shy and reluctant to talk unless prompted. She is of the view that the key issues are:

1. Anxiety attacks resulting from appointments to sites Mr. Whibley has not attended before.
2. Anxiety attacks concerning longer drives (over 30-40 miles).
3. Flashback episodes.
4. A significantly reduced social life.
5. Mr. Whibley has given up playing golf
6. Since 21 June 2014 Mr. Whibley has not touched any form of alcohol despite previously being a keen wine drinker.

(2.2) PREVIOUS PERSONAL HISTORY

Mr. Whibley was born in North Yorkshire and grew up there until he attended university in Aberyswith. He is an only child and generally has good memories of his childhood. His father passed away in when Mr. Whibley was in his early 20's and he has remained close to his mother. He sees her infrequently and she is now in poor health herself and resides in a care home in North Yorkshire.

Mr. Whibley enjoyed school and university and has pursued a professional career in engineering. He describes being happy in his job but does express some regret that he did not pursue some potential opportunities overseas.

Mr. Whibley has been married since 1987 and he appears to have a very close and loving relationship with his wife. They do not have any children.

(2.3) PREVIOUS MEDICAL HISTORY

Mr. Whibley described his medical history noting that from a reasonably young age (late 20's) he had been diagnosed with hypertension. This has been medicated with Perindropol and Doxasosin for nearly 30 years and appears to be controlled. Mr. Whibley currently takes 8 mg of Perindropol daily 2 mg Doxasosin daily and 400 mg of Allopurinol daily for gout. None of these medications note any hallucinatory/psychotic side effects either individually or in combination. Mr. Whibley did not note any previous psychological problems and history of such in his family. There is no history of taking any psychotropic medication and neither has Mr. Whibley undergone any psychological therapy prior to 21 June 2014. Since then however Mr. Whibley had a session of appointments with a counsellor he attended five sessions in all but did not find this of any help commenting that generally the counsellor just let him talk about the events of 21 June the subsequent flashbacks and anxiety attacks and his feelings and thoughts around the whole event and experience. Mr. Whibley felt if anything these sessions had made things worse rather than better and Mrs. Whibley agreed with this. Mr. Whibley is understandably skeptical about the benefits of these sessions but he wishes to try and establish what exactly happened to him that evening.

(2.3.1) MEDICAL RECORDS

Mr. Whibley's general practice records from 1981 onwards have been obtained and studied by me in respect of references to psychological or psychiatric symptoms/conditions which predate the matter under litigation or occur subsequent to it and which may be relevant to the current investigation.

(a) PRIOR TO THE INCIDENT

July 1969 – father passed away and seeks medication to deal with anxiety and lack of sleep

November 1986 – sleeping issues reported but refuses medication

January 2003 – reports mild anxiety attacks as a result of deterioration in mother's health. She is placed in a care home. Amotriplin prescribed for three months. Mr. Whibley notes that he only took the medication for just under three weeks as he was concerned about addiction.

February 2007 – describes stress at work as a result not sleeping – been going on for months. Reluctant to take medication.

April 2010 – complains of feeling "lethargic and low" – sent to consultant, various test undertaken. Blood pressure high – possible anxiety noted – Perindropol dosage increased from 4 mg to 6 mg daily.

(b) SUBSEQUENT TO THE INCIDENT

June 2014 – GP makes initial home visit – prescribed Amotriplin. Possible PTSD/psychosis noted in records.

July 2014 – GP recommends counselling and refers to psychologist.

October 2014 – sessions with psychologist cease and preliminary report identifies possible PTSD/psychosis – possibly drug induced.

(2.4) TEST RESULTS
(2.4.1) DSM-IV POST TRAUMATIC STRESS DISORDER SYMPTOM CHECKLIST
(As compiled by the writer from the above interview)

A (1) Event involving actual/threatened death, serious injury or threat to physical integrity NO

(2) Experience of intense fear, helplessness or horror?

Symptom present

Current post accident but not necessarily current

B RE-EXPERIENCE PHENOMENA

(1) Recurrent/intrusive recollection YES YES

(2) Recurrent dreams YES YES

(3) Acting/feeling "As If" event recurring NO NO

(4) Distress on exposure YES YES

(5) Physiological reactivity on exposure YES YES

C AVOIDANCE/NUMBING

(1) Avoidance of thoughts/feelings NO NO

(2) Avoidance of activities/situations YES YES

(3) Inability to recall NO NO

(4) Diminished Interest YES YES

(5) Estrangement/detachment YES YES

(6) Constricted affect NO NO

(7) Sense of foreshortened future NO NO

D INCREASED AROUSAL

(1) Sleep difficulties YES YES

(2) Irritability/angry outbursts YES YES

(3) Concentration difficulties NO NO

(4) Hypervigilance YES YES

(5) Exaggerated startle NO NO

For a DSM-IV diagnosis of PTSD, positive answers are required from (A) 1 and 2, a minimum of one symptom from (B), three symptoms from (C) and two symptoms from (D). In addition, there must be clinically significant impairment of functioning.

(YES) Symptom present but not necessarily related to PTSD? Some symptomatology present but does not fulfil criteria.

(3) DISCUSSION AND OPINION

Following a dinner party on 21 June 2014 Mr. Whibley suffered anxiety attacks bouts of sleeplessness flash backs and possible hallucinations.

Mr. Whibley clearly suffered from a hallucinatory episode on the evening of 21 June 2014 and in the early hours of the following day. The numerous sightings of Satan the noose the singer the birth of a child by Ms. Trelewyn-Digby the departure in his car the following morning with Satan and the baby lead me to cautiously suggest that Mr. Whibley experienced a drug induced psychotic episode. If anything the post event counselling made the post event anxiety and sleeplessness worse and there has been very slow improvement in the intensity of his psychological reaction over time.

Prior to 21 June 2014 Mr. Whibley experienced some stress both at work and in certain family issues notably the ill health of his mother and the death of his father. These episodes were short lived and were related to specific fact matters and did not persist for any length of time. Based on all the information available there is no indication of a continuation of a pre-existing condition. The anxiety attacks bouts of sleeplessness flash backs and possible hallucinations all appear to have started after the 21 June 2014. Consequently his symptoms can be entirely attributed to events occurring on the evening in question.

(4) CONCLUSIONS
(4.1) SUMMARY OF DIAGNOSIS

This leads me to a qualified diagnosis of Post-Traumatic Stress Disorder following a drug induced psychotic episode at Rippleswade Hall. Mr. Whibley described significant symptoms of traumatization with a marked sense of vulnerability which underlies his general anxiety.

(4.2) CAUSATION

Mr. Whibley has suffered a drug induced episode of hallucinations that have caused trauma and possible psychosis afterwards. Despite there being no clinical evidence for this there does not appear to be any other plausible explanation for what Mr. Whibley experienced that evening and subsequently. It is highly unlikely that the beginning of a psychotic episode was purely coincidental with the visit to Rippleswade Hall.

(4.3) PROGNOSIS

There has been little improvement to date in Mr. Whibley's symptomatology despite being referred for counselling. However this form of therapy is rarely appropriate in such cases and can conversely make the situation worse. He requires cognitive behavioral therapy and possible psychiatric referral. With appropriate intervention there should be good recovery within two years from the commencement of such.

(4.4) TREATMENT REQUIRED

Mr. Whibley currently requires cognitive behavioral therapy with a therapist such as a chartered clinical psychologist or cognitive behavioral therapist and in addition a consultant psychiatric referral. Both should be sought privately given the long waiting lists within the NHS. The cost of therapy should be budgeted at between £100 and £140 per session. Some two sessions per month for the first 12 months is suggested as reasonable the matter can be reviewed thereafter. A psychiatrist will be able to set out a treatment plan costings and prognosis for the psychosis.

(5) DECLARATION

I understand that my duty as an expert witness is to the court. I have complied with that duty. This report includes all matters relevant to the issues on which my expert evidence is given. I have given details in this report of matters which might affect the validity of this report. I have addressed this report to the court.

I confirm that I have not entered into any arrangement where the amount or payment of my fees is in any way dependent on the outcome of the case.

I confirm that insofar as the facts stated in my report are within my own knowledge I have made clear which they are and I believe them to be true and that the opinions I have expressed represent my true and complete professional opinion.

Mr. T A Carrington BSc. MSc. CPsychol

Chartered Clinical Psychologist

(6) APPENDIX

Diagnostic and Statistical Manual of Mental Disorders (DSM-IV) – 4th ed. (1994)

Published by the American Psychiatric Association

The ICD-10 Classification of Mental and Behavioral Disorders (1993)

By the World Health Organization